Cloudberry Castle

Ballet School Secrets

Cloudberry Castle

Ballet School Secrets

Janey Louise Jones

 Kelpies

Kelpies is an imprint of Floris Books

First published in 2011 by Floris Books

The publisher acknowledges subsidy from
Creative Scotland towards the publication
of this volume.

British Library CIP Data available

ISBN 978-086315-839-1

Printed in Great Britain
by CPI Cox & Wyman

For Angela Watson and her ballerinas,
who have been so helpful.

1. Cloudberry Castle
School of Ballet

I couldn't believe that it was time to move up to the big castle! The Cloudberry Castle School of Ballet was soon to open for business. All my dreams were coming true and I felt like the luckiest girl in the world.

It was last July, and we were all flat-out busy preparing for the move. Dad loved his role as chief project manager up at the castle. He burst into the family kitchen in Holly Cottage one day, shortly before the move.

"Katie and Sorcha, I need two ballerinas! Quickly! That's the ballroom studio just finished this minute! The barre is fitted and the mirrors are up," he said. "You have to test it out."

"Cool!" I said. We hadn't been allowed in there for months. "C'mon, Sorcha. Let's get our ballet things!"

We grabbed our bags, and got in the car with Dad.

He raced over there. We jumped out the minute the car stopped, bombing up the stairs to the ballroom.

It was spectacular.

"Wow!" I gasped. "This is the best ballet studio I've ever seen."

"And is it really ours?" whispered Sorcha.

"Well, yes. But remember, we'll have to share all this with everyone who comes to the ballet school. Let's put some music on," I said.

"Yeah! What are you going to pick?" she asked.

"That's easy – *The Sleeping Beauty*," I said, "*The Entrance of the Good Fairies*. I'll show you what to do!"

Dad watched us proudly as we glided blissfully around the new studio, doing *pirouettes* and *arabesques*.

"Sorcha, follow me," I said. "We'll do an *arabesque* followed by a *battement glissé*. Just copy what I do. That's it. Swish your foot out. Well done!"

"I love dancing in here," said Sorcha. "It's like being in our own fairy tale."

I loved it too – especially having the mirrors to check out my footwork. We spent over an hour in there, perfecting a little *Sleeping Beauty* routine.

Afterwards, Sorcha and I had a look around the castle, taking in the changes.

"Come on, let's check out the bedrooms," I said, charging up to the second floor of the castle.

"Won't the boarding girls miss their families?" asked Sorcha.

"Maybe a little at first. But they're going to be so busy dancing that time will fly," I assured her.

"Ooh, these rooms are so pretty!" said Sorcha.

I had to agree. They were painted in a lovely colour called Ballet Shoe Pink, with some walls covered in pretty paper called Rose Sprig. They are kind of atticy rooms with sloping ceilings. I'd say they were the maids' rooms years ago.

In the middle of the six little bedrooms, there was a huge sitting room, filled with four comfy sofas, one in mulberry velvet, one in lime green linen, and one in bright pink fabric. The final one was a crazy patchwork design, involving loads of bright colours and patterns. We had bought this huge TV in Perth, which was a bit like a cinema screen, and there was a coffee table, plus scatter cushions and some pictures for the walls.

I was so proud of it all. We ambled back to Holly Cottage, discussing the story of *The Sleeping Beauty*. It was a bittersweet time, saying goodbye to our beloved cottage. Our life in Cloudberry Castle was about to begin, but we had been so happy in our tiny family home.

"This is the hardest thing I've ever done," I told Mum, as we browsed through a glossy ballet brochure, filled with pictures of beautiful ballet shoes and fluffy tutus, while

Sorcha drew pictures of ballerinas. Hamish, meanwhile, made a wizard's brew in a bucket in the garden.

"Yes, it's tough for us all, darling. We've been blissfully happy in this little house. But it's a fresh start," said Mum. "And how exciting – I still can't believe it's happening to us. And it's all your doing, Katie!"

"I just can't believe that we're going to have our very own ballet school! I've never been so excited," I said.

"You have worked so hard for this ballet dream to come true, Katie." Mum smiled.

I looked up to Cloudberry Castle. I had a lot to think about, and when I feel that way, I always go and chat to Bella – my lovely little pony. I don't ride her as she's too small, but we're the best of friends. I knew she was in the paddock by the castle, near Lily's Lake.

I pulled on my wellies.

"Mum, I'm going to see Bella," I said.

"Hey, Katie, can I come?" said Sorcha.

"Sure, get ready." I smiled.

We strolled over to the paddock together.

"I don't know if I'm going to like my new room in the castle," said Sorcha.

"Why's that?" I said.

"Oh, just cos the ceilings are really high, plus all my dollies like being on the shelves in my own room in the cottage," she explained.

"And where will you put your dollies in your new room?" I asked.

"I dunno. Maybe Dad will build some shelves just like the old ones, so that the dollies will feel at home," she said.

"I think we should ask Dad to do exactly that," I said, ruffling up her hair.

We saw Bella grazing on the far side of the paddock.

"Bella!" I called. "Come over, girl!"

Instantly, she looked up and began to trot over to us. Lovely Bella!

2. Sleeping Beauty

"Oh, hello Bella," I said, as she nuzzled into me. I pulled up some handfuls of juicy grass for her.

"We're going through so many changes, Bella. But your life isn't going to change, so you don't have to worry. So much has happened in the space of a few months."

Sorcha and I brought her out of the field and we sat under a tree, with the sun beating down on us, as Bella grazed contentedly.

"I'm going to gather a load of strawberries!" decided Sorcha, as she noticed a juicy red crop close to the lake.

"Okay. Be careful!" I said.

Bella listened intently as I told her our story, as if she understood every word of it – and I like to think she did.

"The thing is, Bella, for most of my childhood, I gazed up at the big castle from my attic bedroom window, asking myself what Dr Campbell was doing in there. I guessed he was working on things to do with Egyptology. He loved everything to do with ancient Egypt. And I was so sad when he died. I thought I'd never be happy again. And when we realised he had left the castle to us in his will – it was such a shock!" I stroked Bella's nose, as I recalled all that we had gone through.

"I spent so much time thinking about what would happen if we lost the castle. And we so very nearly did. I fought for this castle, Bella," I told my pony. "And when I found Dr Campbell's last novel in a notebook, I was convinced it would make money for us to do up the castle! And it did!"

She whinnied gently, shaking her mane.

"I'm sure Dr Campbell is proud of me. And I bet he's delighted that the whole Mackenzie family are going to live in the castle. Me, Mum, Dad, Sorcha and Hamish. I can see him smiling in the clouds."

Bella looked up at the sky as I did so, and swished her tail happily at that thought.

"Strawberries!" said Sorcha, returning to my side. "And they're really red, so they'll be super-sweet."

"Lovely. Thanks, sis," I said. We shared them with Bella.

The sun seemed to shine endlessly during our last days in Holly Cottage, and the cottage's garden smelled lovely, with the perfume from the deep pink roses and the ripe, juicy raspberries, which grew in a crazy tangle around the old sundial.

The familiar kitchen seemed to be rich with memories of family meals – Christmases and birthdays, tea parties and Sunday brunches. Mum's chocolate sponge cakes, mince pies, apple crumbles and famous caramel shortcake had all been made at that bashed old table.

All through July and August, Mum sat at the kitchen table, writing notes about her plans for the ballet school. Sometimes she would suddenly get up, and start to *pirouette* and *jeté*, as she thought through a little routine. I'd never seen her dance in the house like that before. Her old self, the prima ballerina in the famous New York City Ballet, came back to life that summer.

"I think the first big show should be *The Sleeping Beauty*," she said, as we washed tomatoes and salad leaves one morning for lunch. "It's one of my all-time favourite ballets."

"I love it too!" I gasped.

"*The Sleeping Beauty* is *really* special," said Mum. "Princess Aurora is a lovely part. The Lilac Fairy too. And then there are the Gold, Silver, Sapphire and Diamond Fairies, plus duchesses, baronesses and marchionesses –

and fairy-tale characters too! Just think of the fun we're going to have! There are just so many wonderful parts for our girls. Yes, that's definitely the one! Let's order some costumes from that gorgeous brochure we've got. I'm sure there is a *Sleeping Beauty* section."

"Oh yes, there is – the tutus and headdresses look so amazing. I'll go and get it!" I said.

When I came back from the family room with the brochure, we sat side by side at the table, browsing and ooh-ing and aah-ing.

"I've never danced *The Sleeping Beauty* before," I said. "Who'll get the main part, d'you think?"

"Darling, if we are going to run Cloudberry as a reputable ballet school, we'll have to hold auditions in the normal way, and have a panel of teachers come to a decision. I'm not sure that other parents would appreciate it if I gave my own daughter all the lead roles," said Mum. "This is the sort of little dilemma we're going to have to get used to."

"Does that mean even if I *was* the best dancer at the auditions, I still might not get the part?" I asked.

"Oh, let's cross that bridge when we come to it," said Mum. "I'll try to be as fair as possible. You trust me to do that, right?"

"Course I do, Mum," I replied.

"Let's fill out this order form here," said Mum. "What

fun to be able to afford a whole room full of exquisite costumes."

"It's the coolest thing in the world. And we can order ballet shoes too, can't we? And ribbons. Oh, and tiaras too. And what about practice-wear too? Crossover cardys, wraparound skirts – let me go and get a pen, and we can mark off everything we like. Then I'll go on the website and we can place the order!" I said.

"Okay, and then we'll make raspberry jam with all the berries in the garden," said Mum. "That way, we can take it with us, and still taste Holly Cottage even after we've left."

At that moment, Sorcha came running past us, being chased by Hamish with a worm in his hand.

3. A Whole New World

By the middle of August, we hardly saw Dad around the cottage. He was practically living at the castle, trying his best to get it perfect for us.

The school was due to open on the 21st of September. We already had a few pupils due to arrive just before then. They had all sent DVDs showing their dancing skills, but Mum was also holding more auditions early in September, for girls who had only just heard about the school.

"We will need a lot more pupils if we're to make enough money to stay open," said Dad. He was always doing the sums and fretting over them.

"Good thing someone is counting the pennies!" said Mum, patting the ballet brochure guiltily. We had gone *crazy* with our order.

I looked at the list of girls enrolled so far. The definite new arrivals were:

Allie Heron from Edinburgh
Polly Crawford from Dundee
Flossie Fletcher from York
Catriona Norton from Glasgow
Eliza Jenkins from Stirling
Millie Donovan from Southport

And as for those coming for auditions:

Tilda Forbes from Aberdeen
Leo McLennan from London
Didi Jones from Cardiff
Mary-Jane Olsen from Oban

I wondered how good all the other dancers might be. Much as I still loved the fact that I had managed to bring my ballet-school dream to life, I couldn't help thinking that I'd given myself a lot of tough competition.

I packed all Hamish and Sorcha's stuff for Mum. Eventually, we got to the stage where we were living around loads of brown cardboard boxes. It was so frustrating – we could never find anything we wanted.

"Mum, where are my blue football shorts?" Hamish asked time after time.

"Sorry, darling," said Mum. "They're in a box, but I don't know which one."

"Mum," said Sorcha, "I can't find my best teddy – don't tell me. He's in a box."

"Sorry, guys," I said. "Maybe I've been a bit *too* organised!"

As the final raspberries ripened and the cloudberries sweetened on the Cloudberry estate, we knew it was time to say our final goodbyes to Holly Cottage.

The last sleep in there was warm and toasty. I could smell the berries in the air and my cranberry-coloured walls held me safe as they always did. At first I didn't want to get up that morning, but then I remembered all that was waiting for us up at the castle and I bounced out of bed and into the shower.

The last breakfast was super-yummy. Mum laid out loads of warm pastries, filled with chocolate, fruit, almond paste and icing, with jugs of fresh orange, as she was too busy to make porridge and wholemeal toast as she usually did.

"This is magic," said Hamish hungrily. "I hope Mum is too busy every day from now!"

Just after breakfast, the doorbell rang; it was the removal men. There were six of them and they picked up the heavy cardboard boxes easily, as if they were empty, and packed them neatly into the back of the big blue van. There were certain things I wanted to carry myself, such as my ballet case and my washbag plus other personal stuff.

"At least we can still visit the cottage," said Mum, as she saw my bottom lip quivering when the removal men had loaded all the boxes into the van.

"I know. Thank goodness Mrs Renton is moving in, and not some total stranger," I said.

"She is going to be a lifesaver!" said Mum. Our lovely family friend and faithful babysitter, Mrs Renton, had decided to rent out her Post Office to her nephew and his wife. She fancied a change of lifestyle, and had agreed to be a sort of Mary Poppins for Sorcha and Hamish. She's one of the only people who can control Hamish.

Once our boxes were taken out, another removal van appeared and Mrs Renton's things were carried in.

Sorcha and I hitched a ride up to the castle on the back of the removal van. When we got into the courtyard, we grabbed our special things, and jumped off the van, running into the castle.

The entrance hallway looked beautiful, all bright and sunny, not dusty and dark like before. There were still all the old ancestral portraits on the walls, but there were modern white coffee tables and bright lime and pink sofas too, so it looked like a lovely mix of old and new things. The reception desk was made from a mixture of glass and very bleached-out wood. Some of Mum's really cool black and white ballet pictures, from when she danced with the New York City Ballet at the Lincoln

Centre, had been blown up into huge posters, which were framed and dotted around the entrance area.

"What d'you think, girls?" asked Dad, standing proudly on the staircase, looking down at us.

"It's cool!" said Sorcha.

"Definitely is, Dad," I said. "Nice job."

"Thanks, girls," he said. "It's all worth it if you guys approve."

"Let's go and check on our bedrooms!" shrieked Sorcha.

4. The Old Nursery

We went through the big new door that now separated the private flat, which was our new home, from the actual school. Everything was so different from before, when Dr Campbell lived there. Mum and Dad had made a great job of having our family flat decorated. The pure white walls looked so fresh and clean, and the lovely cosy rugs, all in rust, dark pink and spice colours, made it look homely.

But there were also still loads of Dr Campbell's things. I noticed some of his favourite paintings hanging up where they were before. Sorcha and I went into the sitting room, which used to be Dr Campbell's library. It looked so big and open, waiting to receive the Mackenzie family furniture, which the removal men had just brought up from Holly Cottage.

The stick Dr Campbell used to poke the fire with was

still hanging at the side of the big, open fireplace. Mum had filled the fireplace with a vase of wild flowers from the estate – delphiniums, hollyhocks and roses. I could imagine him sitting by the fire in his favourite chair, smiling with pride at all we had done to keep the castle in the "family".

My bedroom is one of the first rooms you come to as you enter the flat. Sorcha and I went back along the hall and I opened the door to it.

"Wow! It's huge!" said Sorcha.

"I know. All these years I've been practising ballet in a tiny little room, and now I have a massive bedroom, *plus* my very own ballet school to practise in. We're so lucky, Sorcha."

"Yeah," said Sorcha. "At first I thought it was boring owning the castle, but now that we're going to have our very own ballet school, it's so exciting! It's just a shame I'm too young to go to school here. I'm still going to go to Lochvale Primary every day – how annoying! Just think how much you'll be able to lie in when you wake up in your own school. Come and see my room now!"

I followed her along the hallway. The removal men were busily carrying beds, tables and sofas through the flat.

We got to her room, next door to Mum and Dad's.

"Wow! This is what I call bright pink!" I said, laughing.

"Actually, it's called Candyfloss Girl," said Sorcha proudly.

"Well, it's delicious!" I said.

"I thought I'd put my dollies under the window here – or maybe they'll be cold there? Yes, I'll need to think of something else. Dad never did get round to building some shelves for them," she said.

"I'm sure he will; just give him time," I said. "How about some lunch?"

"Yeah, I'm starving!" said Sorcha. "Mum and Dad hardly remember to cook any more. And we haven't had homemade cakes for ages."

We sat at our familiar kitchen table and chairs, which had just been set down by the removal men. Somehow having our battered old kitchen table in place made everything seem all right.

"Katie, can you keep a secret?" asked Sorcha.

"Sure. What is it?" I said.

"I've found a really special room in the castle. It's at the top of one of the corner towers," she whispered. "The door's hidden behind a curtain."

"Oh, and what's so special about it?" I asked.

"I'll show you after lunch," said Sorcha.

A few minutes later, I followed her out of our flat, onto the main staircase, then through a small door leading onto another slightly smaller staircase. All those times when she'd come over to "help" Dad in the castle certainly meant she knew her way around.

"Here it is!" she said.

"Where?" I asked, not seeing anything except a shabby old velvet curtain.

"I told you. Behind the curtain, there's a door," she said, pulling back the curtain.

Sorcha fiddled with the door for what seemed like ages, and finally opened it wide.

I gasped. It was an old-fashioned nursery, with a rocking horse, a cradle, a rocking chair and an old, wooden baby chair.

The rocking chair was placed by the window. *There must be an amazing view from up here*, I thought, so I went over to have a look. As I stood by the chair, I looked out of the window onto Lily's Lake. I was right: I could see across the whole estate, to Holly Cottage and the village of Lochvale. A ripple ran eerily across the lake, as gust of wind hit the tower, making the window rattle.

I became aware that the chair had started to move.

"Someone's rocking the chair!" I said.

"You must have knocked it," said Sorcha. "How could it rock when there's no one in it? Come on! Let's explore!" said Sorcha. "It's fun."

"Actually, I'd rather get out of here," I said, shuddering.

I was totally creeped out. I swung round towards the

door, and as I did so, I saw a little girl in an old-fashioned, long ballerina dress standing in front of it, blocking my way out. She wore her hair in a bun, with fresh flowers. On her dainty feet were pink ballet shoes. Her eyes were sad, as if she'd been crying. I closed my eyes to get rid of the image. When I opened them, she had gone.

She can't have been real, I thought. *Me and my crazy imagination!*

"We must go now, Sorcha," I said.

"Aw, we haven't even played with anything," she complained.

I couldn't get out of that nursery quickly enough.

5. Tilda

Once we had been living in the flat in the castle for a week, we felt almost at home there. Now, it was time for the School of Ballet to come to life.

First of all, we needed more pupils than those who had already enrolled, and the potential new girls began to arrive for auditions. They all looked lovely. I guess that girls who are into ballet have a kind of connection together and like the same hairstyles and clothes, because I thought that all the girls who came were great.

Mum set up auditions in the ballroom dance studio, and she was busy for a while, looking at dancers, talking to them, and working out if they would be able to stay away from home.

I joined Mum in her new office behind reception one morning.

"Katie, we didn't want you to go away to school, so

we have to imagine how tough it is for these families, thinking about their girls coming to ballet boarding school," she said.

"We'll just have to try really hard to make them all feel at home," I said. "As long as we're kind and helpful, surely it'll all work out?"

"Yes," said Mum. "But the only thing is that we also have to be firm. Children need a lot of love and warmth, but also rules and boundaries. We don't want chaos at Cloudberry. I've been thinking about this. We need to work out if you should sleep in our flat with the family, or share the upstairs bedrooms with your new friends. You might feel more involved if you sleep with the other girls, and stay in the flat in the holidays. That way, you can help everyone to settle in, plus they won't get the idea that you're getting special treatment by staying with your own family."

"Hmm. I'll have a think about that," I replied. I hadn't imagined that I wouldn't be welcome to sleep in my own lovely new bedroom.

"Gosh, look at the time. I must fly!" said Mum, draining her mug of coffee and dashing along to the ballroom studios.

I watched her disappear down the corridor.

She looked lovely. She had ordered all these new ballet outfits for her new role as Head of Dance. She wore a pretty white long-sleeved leotard, with a pink overskirt, pink tights and black ballet flats. Her hair was pulled into a soft bun, with wispy sections hanging down here and there.

I sat at her desk and thought about my wonderful new bedroom. It would be so tough, living out of my own family house in a boring old "dorm". But, then again, Mum was right – I might look very smug if I was able to go into my own room every night. I decided to block the problem out of my mind for now.

Didi Jones and Mary Jane Olsen came for trial days, but Mum didn't think they were quite right for Cloudberry. Didi was very shy and Mum felt she would be hopelessly homesick, while Mary Jane was confident, but not the best ballet dancer. She fell over her own feet three times in the audition!

But one morning, a lovely girl with flame-red hair arrived to try out – Tilda Forbes from Aberdeen. I was helping the new caretaker, a young man called Johnny Pickles, to polish the handrail on the central staircase, when Tilda showed up at reception with her mother.

She was pretty, all bright red curls, sunny smiles and freckles. She was quite short in height, and perhaps a little rounded, but so gorgeous, warm and friendly looking that I just knew straight off that I was going to really like her. She was wearing a huge dusky rose-pink flower in her hair, jeans and a sweet white blouse, embroidered round the neckline.

I went down to the reception desk to greet her, as her mum gave various details to Dad, who had agreed to be the receptionist for now. "Why don't you stick a tutu on me and I'll dance the Sugar Plum Fairy as well?" he'd said.

"Hi there," I said to Tilda. "I'm Katie Mackenzie. Welcome to Cloudberry."

"Hey, Katie. Thanks. I'm Tilda. It looks awesome here so far," she said.

"I'd love it if you joined. We need loads of new girls," I said.

"I just hope we can afford it. I love to dance more than anything," she said.

"Me too. I'm totally obsessed with ballet. In fact, I sort of forced my mum and dad into opening this ballet school," I said.

"Wicked. How did you manage that?" she said.

"Let's sit up on the window seat," I said.

We took off our shoes and sat up on a window cushion in the entrance hallway, with our backs to the shutters and our feet touching.

"It's a long story," I began.

"I'd love to hear *all* of it," she said. "I adore stories. I make them up all the time!"

6. Mum's Meltdown

I was still nattering away to Tilda when Mum arrived to show her up to the studios for her audition.

"Mrs Mackenzie, can Katie come too?" asked Tilda.

"Sure, as long as you don't mind," said Mum. "We don't want any overly shy ballerinas. The bigger the show-off, the better!"

"Ah well, you'll not be disappointed with our Tilda then," said her mother, smiling.

We had such fun up in the studio. Tilda's dancing was lovely, but she also giggled and grinned the whole time, which had a sort of infectious effect on me and Mum, so we had the best imaginable time. Tilda stopped every so often to tell us some story about this time when she giggled in a ballet exam, or that time when she did a cartwheel at the end of her dance even though she wasn't supposed to!

Finally, we gave her a tour of the whole castle. I walked with her out to the car as she left.

"We could have a lot of fun here," said Tilda. "Imagine exploring the castle after dark! Does it have dungeons?"

"I'm not sure. I've never gone down any lower than the old kitchens," I said. "But I do know there's something creepy about one room in here – the old nursery."

"Do you think it might be haunted?" asked Tilda.

"Um ... maybe. I'm not completely sure." I hadn't dared to think that there might really be a ghost up there. "Please don't mention this to anyone," I said, playing it down.

"Wow! I hope it is. That'd be cool. I'm a sort of ghost-buster. Really, I've scared off loads of ghosts before," said Tilda.

I laughed nervously. I so hoped that Tilda had made the grade at the audition. She was going to be a good friend to have in the creepy old castle.

Over the next few days, Mum became really stressed out.

"Dan, you've got to help me!" she said one morning, as we all ate sponge cake and custard for breakfast, as there was nothing else in the fridge.

32

"It's rubbish when Mrs Renton goes to Edinburgh to visit her sister," said Hamish. "She makes the best food in the world. I love her French toast with cinnamon. And her porridge is way nicer than Mum's."

"Well, I'm sorry about my terrible food, Hamish," snapped Mum. "I'm just too busy to cook at the moment. I'm trying to open a ballet school here, in case you hadn't noticed."

"Who cares about ballet?" said Hamish. "It would've been better if we had opened a racing track, where we could drive off-road vehicles, and crash them. *BANG!* And then get back in them, all beaten up and then skid them on two wheels..."

By this time, Hamish had two of his toy cars and was acting out the sort of activities he would have preferred at Cloudberry, so that was the end of getting his attention.

"Seriously, Dan," said Mum. "I'm just not coping here. I've still got to unpack all these boxes, work out a course for the dancers, give instructions to the staff. And somewhere in all of this, I'm still a mother to three children – two of whom have not been bathed in a week!"

"Hurray," said Hamish. "I hate washing. I hope that Mum is busy *forever*!"

"Beth, I'm sorry that you're over-stretched," said Dad. "But I don't have enough hours in the day either. If the kitchens and bedrooms don't pass the health and safety inspections on Friday, then we won't be able to open for business at all. I've got a plumber who claims he's stuck in Tenerife, as his holiday firm has gone into liquidation, and I've got an electrician who says he won't work another day until I pay him £12,000. Only, I don't think we owe him that much."

"I know, I know. It's as bad for you as it is for me. But I'm going to snap. I've got to spend some time with the kids," said Mum tearfully.

"Well, why don't you get an assistant? That's what you need. A girl who's a successful ballerina, but who's looking for a bit of teaching experience? I'm sure you know where to approach someone like that? I would kind of like to get back to cereal and toast in the mornings," said Dad.

"Hmmm. That's not a bad idea, Dan," said Mum. "Maybe I'll ask someone at the Scottish Ballet in Glasgow if they know of anyone who would help us for the first term."

Mum jumped off her chair and picked up her computer. "Tomorrow, family, we will eat like normal people! I'm going to e-mail Scottish Ballet and then the supermarket for home delivery!"

"Order a pile of those yummy pastries!" called Hamish.

7. Willow

Later that day, we had a phone call to say that a ballerina from the Scottish Ballet, called Willow Aitken, was looking for teaching experience.

"She's arriving on Friday for a two-week trial, and if it all works out well, she'll stay with us until the Christmas show," said Mum chirpily at teatime. A proper tea – eggs, beans, sausages and hot buttered toast.

"Sounds great, Mum!" I said.

"Yay! And we have loads of new food in the larder. It's a miracle!" said Sorcha.

I caught her and Hamish after tea, taking a secret stash of cupcakes, cartons of fruit juice, yoghurts and mini-cheeses to their rooms.

"For an emergency," said Sorcha.

"A good idea!" I said, with a wink.

The castle was beginning to fill up with people and their stuff, especially as so many of the full-time staff had to live in with us. The Cloudberry family just kept getting bigger and bigger.

We welcomed the new cook, a rosy-cheeked, plump, pretty lady called Mrs Mathers, with open arms. For the first few days, while she was trying out the ovens and kitchen equipment, the most wonderful smells wafted through the castle. Sorcha and Hamish hung out there the whole time.

"Quick!" called Hamish one day. "I've heard Mrs Mathers has made New York brownies. They smell lovely! This is brilliant. I'd say she might even be better than Mrs Renton. But Mrs Renton is better at crafts and putting on voices when she's reading stories. I've got loads of brilliant granny-people now."

"Hamish, you're very sensible to say good things about *all* your granny-people," I said. "Because if they think you have a favourite 'granny', they might get upset."

"I know that, silly," said Hamish.

Mrs Mathers had come recommended by the owner of the hotel in Lochvale and she didn't disappoint us. As well as the most wonderful goodies such as rocky-road squares and fudge, she made tasty dishes like homemade pizzas, creamy risottos, golden pies and the fluffiest mashed tatties in the whole world. She baked bread which melted in the mouth, and yummy desserts too, like upside-down puddings, baked Alaska and crusty apple roll.

"I'll not have any of that fashionable under-eating in this school," said Mrs Mathers over dinner in the new dining room one night, a bit before we opened. "My girls will be well fed and will have a nice bit of roundness about them – something to fall back on if a nasty autumn bug should strike! Some of these ballerinas are far too thin. It doesn't look nice, you know!" she said.

"Quite right, Mrs M," said Dad, tucking into a second portion of her tasty cottage pie.

No sooner had we got used to Mrs Mathers' cheerful rosy face about the place, than we had the excitement of another new arrival. I will never forget the first time I set eyes on Willow Aitken. Dad and I had been away at the Cash and Carry in Perth, getting a huge list of things for Mrs Mathers, and when we got back, Willow was chatting to Mum in the front drawing room.

She sat in one of the new purple velvet chairs, which seemed to frame her perfectly. Her dark hair was glossy and full and moved about beautifully as she gently tossed her head when she spoke. Her wide, violet eyes twinkled and her rosebud lips, which were painted warm pink, always seemed ready to break into laughter. I loved her clothes too. She wore a pretty ivory top and great jeans, along with purple patent ballet pumps. And her handbag was amazing – a big green leather bag, with loads of buckles and stitching. Willow Aitken had to be the coolest girl I'd ever seen.

"Hi Katie!" said Mum, catching sight of me standing by the door. "Come and meet Willow. D'you remember, we actually saw her in the production of *Cinderella* in Glasgow? Such a wonderful dancer!"

"Oh, yes. Were you Cinderella?" I said.

"Yes, I was, Katie. I love doing the big ballets. But long-term, I'd like to have my own ballet school, so teaching is going to be such a good experience," she said.

We sat chatting in the drawing room for ages. Mum left us to it, as she had to make some phone calls about the auditions.

"Katie, can you show Willow the staff bedrooms please?" said Mum. "That's if you'd like to stay the night, Willow?"

"Sure, I'm going to give it a try here and see if I can be of any help to you." She smiled.

"I'm sure you'll be invaluable," said Mum. "I'll ask Johnny to carry your cases up to your room. And I'll just get your keys, so you can lock up your stuff. We don't envisage anything going missing, but you just never know."

"Thanks, Beth," said Willow.

She was the easiest person to talk to; I felt as though I could tell her anything.

"So, Katie," she said. "This place looks absolutely amazing. You guys have done such a great job!"

"Thanks. My mum and dad have been flat out busy for months," I said.

"But I heard from your mum that you were the one who really wanted to start the ballet school," she said.

I nodded, blushing. It seemed a bit bratty when I came to think of it.

"C'mon," I said, "I'll show you round the castle."

8. Coppélia

First of all, we went up to the staff bedrooms, which were close to the girls' bedrooms, but separated by two heavy doors.

"So, this would be your room, I guess," I said, showing Willow into the brightest of the staff rooms.

Dad had made sure that every part of the castle was as good as our own flat on the first floor. The walls of Willow's room were painted sage green, and there were matching curtains at the window. The bed looked very comfortable, with a white and green throw across it. There was a private shower room attached, and plenty of cupboard space for clothes and personal belongings.

"I like it!" said Willow. Johnny appeared with her two suitcases.

"Would you like me to leave you to unpack?" I said.

"No, not at all. I can do that later. I'd love to see the rest of this place, it's just awesome!"

Willow grabbed her bag, locked her door, and we checked out all the main places together – the dining room, the normal classrooms and the kitchens. I left out the creepy old nursery room at the top of the tower. "Now let's see the actual ballet bits of the castle," I said.

"Sure, I've brought my ballet shoes, so we can have a spin," she said.

First, we looked at the theatre, and then the costume room, plus the changing rooms.

"And now for the ballet studios!" I said. "The ballroom makes such a great studio base. The three little studios all join up to make one huge studio, or can be partitioned off into three for separate classes."

"This is amazing," she said. "I've never seen anything of this standard in a ballet school. Cloudberry Castle is going to be respected across the world. You must be so proud," she said.

"I am, but it still hasn't really sunk in yet. I suppose I'm just dying for all the girls to arrive and for all the dancing fun to begin."

"Why don't we have a dance together now?" she said.

"That would be cool. I think I have a pair of ballet shoes by the piano in here," I said.

Willow took her ballet shoes out of her bag and

slipped them on, tying the ribbons expertly.

"Some music?" I suggested.

"Yes, of course. You choose, Katie," she said.

I put on some classical ballet music, from Coppélia –
Act 2 – *Musiques des Automates.*

"Ah, lovely. I like this," she said.

We both began to glide across the floor, dancing a duet
of Coppélia and Swanhilde, sensing the timing perfectly.
I had never danced with a professional dancer before –
except Mum, of course. We did steps *en arrière* and even
an *arabesque penchée.*

When the music came to an end, we both flopped on
the studio floor.

"Hey Katie, you're an amazing dancer," she said. "I
was nothing like as good as you at the same age."

"Wow, that's such a lovely thing to say, Willow.
Thanks," I said. "I'm going to learn so much from you."

As I helped to untie the ribbons on Willow's ballet
shoes, I suddenly noticed Mum watching from the door.

"Hey, Mum. How long have you been standing there?"
I asked.

"A while." She smiled. "What a lovely dance. Quite
enchanting."

So far, everyone who had arrived to join the Cloudberry family was lovely. But the very next day, somebody totally different arrived for an audition.

"A man in a hat is driving a huge car into the courtyard!" called Sorcha from her favourite nosy-parker point at the hall window.

"Ah," said Mum. "That'll be Leo McLennan. Apparently she's the most amazing dancer. Her mother sent me a DVD of Leo in *The Nutcracker*. It was quite wonderful. Oooh! This is getting really exciting!"

"It's hard to tell from a DVD how good someone is," I commented moodily.

"Believe me, Katie," said Mum. "This girl has something special. I must get down to greet her."

I watched with Sorcha as Leo got out of the car. My goodness, she was so pretty – blonde hair in a bun and the sweetest little doll face imaginable.

"She's really lovely!" I said.

Sorcha peered out of the window. "She's pretty, but she looks very mean," she said. Then she went off to colour in a fairy princess.

9. Dancing Diva

I was really curious about Leo after the way Mum had raved on about her. As Mum had allowed me to be in on Tilda's dance audition, I hoped I'd be allowed into Leo's as well.

I went out of the flat and sneaked into the ballroom, where I practised *pliés* at the barre until Mum and Leo appeared for the dance test.

"Oh, hello Katie," said Mum. "This is Leo."

"Hi Leo. Welcome to Cloudberry," I said.

"What grade are you?" asked Leo.

"Er, grade five," I said.

"Did you get a distinction?" she said.

"Yes," I replied.

Leo put her nose in the air and sat down to change into her ballet shoes.

"Katie," said Mum. "I'll be seeing Leo dance in five minutes. Are you staying or not?"

"I'd like to stay, if Leo doesn't mind," I said.

"I don't care," she replied.

A crowd of people arrived in the ballroom – Leo's mother, her aunt and grandmother, plus a poor lady who carried all the bags and fussed around the family, and the chauffeur too.

"Hello, I'm Mrs McLennan," said her mother, a thin woman with very blonde hair and lots of heavy make-up.

"Ah yes, hello," said Mum. "Very pleased to meet you."

"You do know that Leo has special dietary requirements, don't you? And we must have the pony stabled here if she's to come to Cloudberry. Can we see the stable block afterwards?"

"Yes, that will all be fine," said Mum. "I'll take you over there myself."

I was shocked – I had no idea that we were going to agree to stable ponies at Cloudberry. What if every girl brought a pony? I couldn't believe that Mum was okay with such a thing. It seemed as if Leo was the ultimate spoiled brat.

It was so strange to hear Mum being so professional and remote, not like Mum at all, more like one of my teachers at my old school in the village.

I admit I was intrigued by Leo, even though I didn't like her much. Everything about her seemed better than anyone else. And yet, why did I think that? So far my impression of Leo came from her attitude; I didn't know what she was really like yet.

There was such a fuss when it came to playing her chosen piece of music.

"This is a fairy dance which I have choreographed myself," she announced.

The music was delicate and enchanting. Leo was not content with simply changing shoes; she disappeared for a few moments and came back in a lovely pale pink fairy tutu.

"It's from The Ballet Boutique in New York!" she declared.

She danced like a butterfly, all dainty steps and beautiful jumps. Her timing was perfect and her range of moves amazing for her age – including a *grand battement en cloche*. There was so much emotion in her face, and her hand movements were the most graceful I'd ever seen. She was in a league of her own. It gave me a pain in my heart to admit it, but Leo was a much better dancer than me. When she danced, everything about her became real, sincere and convincing.

When the music came to an end, she curtseyed. The smug expression came back over her face, and she was instantly annoying again.

But Mum was delighted with her, of course.

"That was wonderful, Leo. Rarely, if ever, have I witnessed such a dancer. It's a privilege to see you dance. We would be thrilled if you would come to Cloudberry. This is just the sort of standard we need to set," said Mum.

"We will discuss your offer," said Mrs McLennan. "As you can imagine, Leo could go to any ballet school we choose. But what we like about this place is the stables. She cannot live without The Duke. And if you could accommodate him, then that would really swing things for us."

That sounded a lot like a threat to me – if we didn't take The Duke, then we couldn't have Leo.

10. New Rules

"Let me take you over to the stables right now," said Mum. "My daughter Katie stables her pony Bella there. But Bella is not a fancy pony – she's a chubby little thing!"

Huh! A chubby little thing? How mean to say that about faithful little Bella. She's easily the cutest pony in the world.

I couldn't bear to go over to the stables, and listen to them laugh at poor old Bella. And worse, to hear Mum laughing with them. I went back to our flat and read one of my Sadler's Wells books.

When Mum came back, she was full of chat about Leo.

"Oh Dan!" she said, as she portioned out a delicious looking lasagne made by Mrs Mathers. "You should see this girl. She would really put us on the map. I know she'd be great for us. And to think, she could have a place at any dance school in the country, if not the world. Yet, she may well come to Cloudberry!"

I'd had just about enough of all this fuss about Leo McLennan. This wasn't how I'd imagined my dream dance school to be.

Mum came into my room later that night to say goodnight, as she always did.

"So, what did you think of that girl today?" she asked casually.

"Very good," I replied.

"I really think she's quite exceptional. It's so exciting. She could easily be the next prima ballerina of her generation!" said Mum.

I felt my bottom lip tremble. It's not that I think I always have to be the best, it's just that I want my own mum to think I'm the best.

"But you're still my favourite dancer, darling," she said. "It's just that I have to think in terms of the business now."

"I understand," I said. And I did understand, but it hurt me nonetheless.

I slept badly that night. I was hot and restless, imagining strange noises and shadows. I opened my eyes at one point to see the little ballerina girl from the old nursery at the bottom of my bed. She wore the same long, old-fashioned ballet dress, and fancy floral headdress. *Maybe she's a character from one of my books about Sadler's Wells*, I thought. I leaned forward and reached out to touch her. She had looked so real, but there was no one there.

It all seemed so silly by morning and I put it down to a bad dream. *Me and my daft imagination!*

At the beginning of September, just when Cloudberry was beginning to look a tiny bit autumnal, with the first copper leaves on the big old beech trees on the driveway, it was time for the girls who had passed their auditions to arrive at Cloudberry Castle School of Ballet.

The night before they started to arrive, I strung up a homemade "welcome" banner in the shared sitting room for the girls, and I put little vases of fresh wild flowers in all the rooms.

"I so want them to feel welcome," I told Sorcha, who was my assistant in the flower arranging.

"D'you think you'll like all the girls, Katie?" asked Sorcha, as we sat side by side on one of the new sofas in the girls' sitting room.

"Most of them. But I'm worried about one of them – Leo," I admitted.

"Told you she's mean," said Sorcha. "You can see it in her eyes."

"I'm going to have to get along with her, though," I said. "For Mum and Dad's sake. And for the sake of Cloudberry."

Tilda Forbes was due to arrive one day soon, before everyone else, as it suited her family better that way. I couldn't wait for her to show up. It was time for the ballerinas to dance through the castle!

"Oh look, Sorcha!" I said, peeking out of the nosy-parker window the next morning. "It's my friend Tilda arriving in a minibus! She's soooo lovely. I want to take her up to her room!"

I ran down to meet the bus.

"Hi, Tilda!" I said.

"Hey, Katie. I'm so totally excited about being here," she said.

I looked with amazement at the amount of people who had come to see her into her new school – her mum and dad, her four brothers and sisters, her two grannies and her Auntie Morag. Quite a crew, but they were all lovely – unlike Leo's entourage – and they made me even surer that Tilda was going to be the easiest person in the world to get along with.

I thought she might be sad when her family left, but she wasn't.

"They'll be back soon," she said confidently.

Johnny took her bags upstairs and we wandered around the castle, enjoying the fact that we had it all to ourselves – for now.

We went into the theatre room and sat in the seats, chatting about all the ballet shows we had performed in.

"Can I try out the stage?" she asked.

I knew we weren't allowed to, but I wanted to impress Tilda. It would be so embarrassing if all the girls thought I was a goody-goody, just because my parents were in charge.

"Um ... yeah," I said. "Let's sneak on to the stage and pretend we're performing."

I put on some pop music and we found some ballet shoes.

"Let's dance like they do on TV," I said.

We got really carried away, jumping around and doing our favourite routines, and we fell about laughing when the music stopped.

"Katie, what's going on?" said Dad, from the double doors leading into the theatre room.

"Sorry, Dad. I just wanted to try out the stage," I said, taking all the blame.

"This theatre hasn't passed its health and safety checks yet. You've no right to be in here. I'm so disappointed in you, Katie. We're relying on you to set a good example to the others," he said.

I had a flashback to the happy days, not so long before, when I secretly slipped into the castle and danced alone, completely free. But Dad still wasn't done with me.

"It's not your dance school you know – you're only a pupil here," he said.

I was so embarrassed. *Tilda must think I'm an idiot.*

I ran out to the hallway in tears, leaving poor Tilda standing on the stage.

"It was all my fault, Mr Mackenzie," I heard her say.

I ran to my bedroom in the family flat. I was hurt, humiliated and really angry.

Why did he speak to me like that? I thought. *If it wasn't for me, there would be no Cloudberry Castle School of Ballet at all.*

11. The Statue

I sobbed into my pillow until it was soaked.

Sorcha came to see what was wrong with me.

"Go away!" I screamed. "I've had it with this family. I wish I'd never suggested the stupid ballet school."

"I don't even know why you did!" she shouted back.

She left the room, looking very worried – poor little lamb.

After a while, I dried my eyes and went to find Tilda, who was unpacking in her room. I didn't want her to think I was the sort of girl who would go off in huge sulks for whole days.

"Hey Tilda. I'm sorry about my dad telling us off like that. He's been a bit stressed out lately. I guess we shouldn't have gone on the stage."

"No, I'm the one who should apologise; it was my idea. Let's just forget about it."

"Once you've finished unpacking, d'you fancy coming for a walk in the grounds?" I said. "I'll show you my pony – but I'll have to check with Dad that it's okay first."

"That sounds brilliant!" she said.

Dad said it was fine, as long as we stayed around the stable and were no more than half an hour. The sun was shining, and we set off round the edges of Lily's Lake and stopped in to check on Bella.

"Can we take her for a walk on her halter?" said Tilda. "My friend's pony loves doing that."

"Oh, okay then, she does look like she wants to get out and about," I agreed.

We ambled around the lake with Bella, walking through avenues of trees and along wild pathways.

We chatted about everything from ballet leotards, to parents, to dividing fractions – something we both detested.

"Look!" said Tilda. "There's a cute little bridge going over this part of the lake. What's over the bridge?"

"Actually, I've never been over that bridge before," I said. "Mum says I mustn't go over it. It's not that strong. And with Dad going crazy this morning, I guess we'd better not try it. I don't want him to freak out again."

"Oh, come on," urged Tilda. "No one's looking. I'll take the blame this time if we get caught! It's so intriguing."

"Oh, I suppose so," I agreed, reluctantly. After the scene from earlier, I didn't want Tilda to think I was a complete wimp. I looked around. It was perfectly quiet, and as far as I knew Mum and Dad hadn't installed CCTVs all over the place – so I thought it was worth the risk.

We tied up Bella at a fence, and made our way towards the wobbly little bridge, which looked as if it was made from nothing stronger than driftwood and rope.

"I'll go first," said Tilda.

I followed on behind her. The bridge shook and swayed, and I was sure we were going to fall straight into the water.

We both gasped with relief when we reached the other side.

"It's so beautiful over here!" said Tilda. "Like an enchanted, secret world. The flowers are lovely. Let's explore."

Birds chirped, while the sun shone through the autumn leaves. I was excited, but also terrified, as I followed Tilda along some tiny paths which led to the centre of the little island.

But Tilda being Tilda didn't want to stick to the paths. She danced through the long grasses and wild flowers, circling round and round like a ballerina from a music box.

She pushed her way through dense bushes and ivy, and I helplessly followed her, trying to enjoy the adventure as best I could.

The foliage was up to our waists and I spotted something straight ahead.

"Look!" I said. "There's some kind of a statue in the middle of all these roses. Let's go and see it."

As we got nearer to the dainty little statue, we couldn't quite believe our eyes.

"Wow, it's a pretty little ballerina!" said Tilda.

"Oh my goodness. I had no idea this was here!" I said, staring at the girl, terror-stuck. She was the same girl I'd seen in the old nursery, and in my dreams. How could it be? I'd never seen the statue before.

Who is she? I asked myself. None of it made sense. I could no longer dismiss the visions as figments of my imagination.

"Let's go up close," said Tilda. "Oooh, I love mysteries like this!"

We held back the roses, but as we made our way closer to the statue, there was a mad flapping of wings in the bushes.

"Aaarrgh! It's bats!" I cried, stumbling, before running back towards the bridge.

Tilda followed me. "It wasn't bats, it was just birds!" she said. "Come on. Let's go back to the statue."

"No, my parents will go crazy and I'm totally spooked now," I said. "We can come back with an adult some other time."

"Okay," said Tilda. "But I think it's really weird that Cloudberry has this ballerina statue, and then you came along and had the idea of turning it into a ballet school. It's dead spooky!"

"Ooh, don't say that, Tilda. I hate creepy things," I said.

And yet, something told me that the castle and ballet did go together in some mysterious way that I had always understood.

"She looked so pretty, didn't she?" said Tilda. "But let's not tell anyone about her. It can be our secret."

I nodded in agreement.

"Your dad's a bit grumpy," said Tilda, as we walked back up to the castle.

"Oh, he's not normally like that, I promise. I think it's because he's in charge of you on behalf of your parents – and my parents take that sort of stuff very seriously. I suppose you can understand how scary it must be – suddenly in charge of all these girls," I said.

"That's nice that you're defending him," said Tilda. "That means you're a proper family. You can shout at each other, but an outsider can't criticise you. That's lovely."

12. Ballerinas

The next day, the other girls arrived and Mum held a little meeting to welcome everyone in the drawing room. She wanted to introduce them to the staff, the Mackenzies and generally tell them the routine of school life here at Cloudberry. Mrs Mathers had made some delicious fairy cupcakes with cloudberry and white chocolate icing for the occasion.

I held Mum's clipboard with the list of girls, and I smiled at everyone as they arrived. I was curious to read the little notes she had made beside each name.

Allie Heron from Edinburgh. Lovely dancer.
Very shy.
Polly Crawford from Dundee. Confident, quite
tall already. Hope she doesn't grow too
much!

Flossie Fletcher from York. Dainty and
sweet. Elegant steps.
Catriona Norton from Glasgow. Wonderful
personality. Dances well.
Eliza Jenkins from Stirling. A big talent
lurks there, but could be a rebel.
Millie Donovan from Southport. Wonderfully
tidy ballet work and sweet disposition.
Jennifer Barnes from Haddington. Sure
footed, lovely character.
Phoebe Yates from Carlisle. Talented, team
player.
Annie Jenkins from Pitlochry. All rounder,
strong grade five skills.
Leo McLennan from London. AMAZING!!!
Star quality.

Tilda and I sat together in the drawing room while
Mum and Dad set out the rules. Since Dad's outburst
about the theatre incident, I realised that I had to take
in the rules just like everybody else, or maybe even more
so. I still had a hard decision to make – was I going to
sleep in the family flat, or with the girls in the school
bedrooms?

"We want you all to enjoy your time here at
Cloudberry," said Mum. "But we need you to stick to

certain routines and obey certain rules. Each day, you will be taught a mixture of academic subjects and ballet classes. You may not, at any time, go out of the castle after lights out. You must never go over the wooden bridge across the lake, nor may you go into any private rooms in the castle. So long as you stick to the rules, we will all get along famously. Now, allow me to introduce you to our resident ballet teacher, Willow Aitken from the Scottish Ballet!"

A ripple of delight ran through the room.

"The Scottish Ballet! Wow!" said one girl.

"I've heard of her before!" gasped another.

After the girls got over their surprise about the ballet teacher, they were keen to tuck into the cupcakes.

"Oh, that reminds me," said Mum. "Let me introduce you to our wonderful cook, Mrs Mathers, who will take care of your nutritional needs. Step forward, Mrs Mathers."

There was a great cheer, led by Tilda.

I watched all the girls mingling over cakes. *They seem a lovely bunch,* I thought. But one was still missing. Leo McLennan hadn't showed up yet.

After the welcome meeting, I went back to my bedroom in our apartment and sat on my bed. The room didn't have the same memories or atmosphere as my bedroom in Holly Cottage. I made my decision – I was going to sleep in the school part of the castle with the other girls.

Tilda helped me take all my stuff up to the school bedrooms. I could hardly believe I was moving away from the Mackenzie family after all – the very thing I said I didn't want to happen. But they weren't too far away!

That day went by in a blur of girls buzzing about, families carrying trunks and suitcases up to the bedrooms, and people being given tours of the castle, plus filling out paperwork at reception.

Before all the parents went away, we had a tea party laid out in the dining room, and Mrs Mathers had done us proud. There were platters of sandwiches, with all sorts of yummy fillings, such as tuna mayonnaise, chicken salsa and Brie with cranberries, plus sausage rolls and tiny quiches. Oh, and there were dips and dipping chips, with loads of carrots, celery and peppers. There were also bowls of fresh fruit, and the most wonderful Victoria sponge cakes, and of course her famous brownies, which completed any meal by Mrs Mathers.

All the families seemed to get on very well, discussing dancing, admiring the castle itself, and general chit-chat.

"Oh!" said Polly. "Look! There's a man in a funny uniform standing at the door!"

We all swung round to look. He was a driver, wearing a cap and smart blue suit. He carried lots of bags and boxes. In fact, he could hardly see over the top of them. Very soon, Leo McLennan appeared at his side, with a beautiful leather saddle over her arm. She swept into the room. He was her personal driver. Trust Leo to make an entrance.

"Ah, hello, Leo!" said Mum, rushing over to welcome her.

She held out the saddle towards Mum. "Could you take this?" she said. "We've had an appalling journey. Scottish roads are more like pathways."

I looked at the other girls and we did a group "tut".

Somehow an icy chill fell over the room after that, and when Mum rushed off to fetch some special food, just for Leo, the rest of us started chatting and moaning, all wondering why we had to help ourselves to food from the table, while Leo was served with special stuff.

Leo McLennan had arrived at Cloudberry!

13. Pony Wars

After we had all finished eating, the parents began to leave, and there were tears.

"Let's play games in the sitting room!" said Tilda cheerfully, acting like she was an old-timer. "I've brought loads of board games. C'mon, we'll play Pictionary!"

As we all headed up to the bedrooms to wash and change, we saw Mum chatting to Leo in the main hall.

"I'm so sorry that The Duke isn't settling in," said Mum. "Are there any of the other stables in the mews that you like?"

Tilda and I looked at each other and rolled our eyes as Leo whispered to Mum.

"But that's Bella's stable," Mum said. "She's used to that one. I don't know if we could move her. She's very old and she's been living there for a long time."

I fizzed with anger. Leo was clearly asking Mum if The

Duke could go in Bella's stable! Never! There's no way I was going to allow that. Tilda and I crept to the edge of the central landing to hear the conversation better.

"I shan't stay if The Duke can't get the bigger stable. He's way bigger than that little Bella. I mean, the whole block is seriously rubbish compared with what he's used to," complained Leo moodily.

"How come she gets to bring her pony?" whispered Tilda. "No one else has."

"Don't ask me why she gets special privileges," I said. "What Leo wants, Leo gets."

"But your mum is going to make her even worse if she keeps giving her what she wants. That's just teaching her to make more demands – that's what my mum says about my little cousin, Toby. He's a monster because he always gets his own way."

We saw Mum heading off to the stable mews with Leo. Mum placed an arm around her shoulder.

"Leo's going to win about this, I can just tell," said Tilda.

I said nothing. I hoped she was wrong, but I didn't feel confident about it.

Up in the bedrooms, there were arguments about who was going to have to share a room with Leo. Willow was trying her best to keep some kind of order, but she wasn't having any luck persuading the girls, none of whom wanted to buddy with Leo.

"There's absolutely no way I'm rooming with her," said Allie.

"Well, I'm not," said Eliza. "She's awful. I've only seen girls like that in films before. I can't believe how spoiled she is."

"Count me out," said Flossie. "She's more of a brat than my baby sister."

"Snap!" said Millie.

One by one, all the girls paired up into rooms. I sighed. I guessed I was going to get left with Leo.

How come this is nothing like as good as it looked on my business plan? I thought.

Leo came back in from the stables with a smug smile on her face.

"Hey, Katie. I hope you don't mind, but The Duke is stabled in Bella's old stall. It makes sense that way as he's way bigger than Bella. Your mum said it was totally fine," she said.

I couldn't speak as I was so angry. I didn't trust myself to say anything, so I just gave a pained little smile.

"Wait until I see Mum! I wonder how she's going to explain this one away," I muttered to Tilda.

"Do they honestly expect me to share?" said Leo, when she noticed that there were two beds in every room.

"We're all sharing," I said, through gritted teeth.

"But I can't! I'm such a light sleeper. I've always had

66

my own room. There's no way I could stand it. There's no way I can share air. No offence," she said.

I ran down to see Mum. She was working on her laptop at the kitchen table in the flat.

"Katie! I know what you're going to say," she said. "I'm truly sorry about moving Bella. There was nothing I could do. I feel terrible."

14. Special Treatment

"It's not about that," I said. "Well, not *only* about that, even though that's bad enough. She's refusing to share with me now. Says she wants her own room – and her own air! The others are furious with her. Mum, this is serious. Why should she get better conditions than everyone else? What are you going to do about it?"

Mum looked very uncomfortable.

"Maybe you could go as a three with Tilda and Catriona?" suggested Mum nervously.

"I don't believe you're giving in to her stupid demands again!" I said. "It's pathetic."

Dad overheard me raising my voice. I'd never spoken to Mum like that before.

"What's got into you, love?" he said. "Try not to upset your mother when she's already stressed out. This isn't like you!"

"Leave it, Dan," said Mum. "She has reason to be upset with me."

"Anyway," said Sorcha. "Leo's annoying! She's nasty!"

Mum sighed, and for a second, I felt very sorry for her. Dad was right when he said this wasn't like me. I hadn't been sleeping well – thinking about the visions of the little ballerina girl and the statue we'd found. I was sure she must be a ghost, and it was making me really tetchy.

Maybe I should tell them what I saw? But I decided they had enough to worry about, without me adding to their list.

"Leave this issue about Leo with me, darling," said Mum.

"I'll move my bed in with Tilda and Catriona," I sighed. "I don't want to share with Leo anyway."

"Girls are just stupid," said Hamish. "They cry and moan the whole time. It's not fair that we don't have more boys here."

"Gosh," said Mum. "My life's falling apart. I can't remember the last time that I had one of Hamish's friends over to play. Honestly, there aren't enough hours in the day."

Sorcha ran over to hug me.

"D'you have to sleep in the school section?" she asked.

"Yes, sweetie," I replied. "I'm not wanted here."

"That's just not true," said Mum, her voice trembling.

"Please bear with me Katie until I get the hang of this. I think I'll have to give Willow some more authority so I can find the time to be some sort of mother to you lot."

I went back upstairs, where Tilda helped me to move my bed into their room.

"You're better off with us," she said.

I announced to Leo that she could have the room to herself.

"Oh!" she said. "What a relief! Now I can unpack."

She went into the room and banged the door behind her. It was as if she simply didn't notice how rude and offensive she was. I had never met anyone quite like her in my life.

All the girls unpacked then went to play games in the communal sitting room. We lounged around on the sofas, chatting about ballet and clothes.

"What's Leo doing?" asked Eliza.

"I don't know," I said.

"So, we're not good enough for her to join us?" said Polly.

"Yeah. She's a bit of a loner," I said.

"What's that noise coming from her room?" said Tilda. She ran over to listen at the door into Leo's room.

"Sounds like a TV," said Tilda.

We all went over to listen. It was a TV – we could hear *Blue Peter* on it.

"My goodness! She has her own TV and we have to share one in here?" said Allie. "That's so not fair."

"I think it's because she's ill or something," I said. I knew there would be big problems for Mum and Dad if everyone started to protest about Leo. Mum would have to see for herself what a selfish girl she was.

A bell rang when tea was ready.

"It smells lovely!" said Catriona as we all got up from the comfortable sofas in the sitting room where we were playing Pictionary. "D'you know what it is?"

"I think it's cottage pie with peas and carrots," I said. "Followed by apple crumble and custard."

"Yum!" she said.

"I can't eat food like that," said Leo, joining us on the staircase. "I need to have organic meals, like homemade sushi and couscous. I've a lot of allergies. My mum's left a list of what I can eat with Mrs Mathers. I mean, I've got a very delicate system. I've always been this way."

"Ah well, more pie and crumble for us!" said Catriona. "Let's get down to the dining room, I'm starving."

Leo sat at the opposite end of the table from us, even though we all tried our best to chat to her.

"Maybe she's a rubbish dancer. She could be home by the weekend," whispered Tilda.

"I've seen her dance," I said softly.

"And?" said Tilda.

"She's wonderful."

"Darn it. How are we going to get rid of her?"

"Let's give her time to settle in," I said, thinking about Mum and trying to be mature. "Maybe she's just shy."

"I want this! I want that! She doesn't seem very shy to me," said Tilda.

"Let's stop thinking about her," said Eliza. "I have an idea for after lights out. Let's take some marker pens and draw moustaches on all those ugly old portraits on the stairway. It'll be such fun. They can only get better looking!"

I sucked my cheeks in with shock! I couldn't stand by and let them vandalise the castle's heirlooms! But what a bore would I look if I stood in their way?

15. Lily's Things

Tilda saved me from a terrible situation.

"We can't do that, Eliza," she said. "There are pranks, and then there's pure vandalism. What if the marker pen won't come off? Those paintings are, like, hundreds of years old."

"Aw, boring!" said Eliza, who seemed as if she would soon think of another ridiculous prank.

That night, I snuggled into my duvet, trying to find something to be happy about. The opening of Cloudberry Castle School of Ballet had been really hard, not nearly as much fun as I had hoped. Most of all, I was hurt that Mum was too busy to think about my feelings and that Dad just thought I was being difficult.

"You asleep?" asked Tilda.

"No. I'm exhausted, but I can't stop thinking about stuff," I said.

"My mind's going crazy too. I'm thinking about my family. At least yours is just downstairs," said Tilda.

"You're right. I'm feeling too sorry for myself. Are you missing your mum and dad?" I asked.

"Yes. I'm fine in the daytime, but it's hard at night," she said.

"I can imagine. I'm sorry about that," I said.

"Thanks," she replied.

There was a silence.

"Katie," said Tilda.

"Yeah?"

"Want to try and find out more about that statue?" she asked.

"Definitely. I've been thinking about it a lot," I said.

"What statue?" said a voice from under Catriona's covers.

Tilda and I giggled. It was no use keeping a secret from a room-mate. We told her all about the ballerina statue on the island in the middle of the lake.

"Cool. I love mysteries," said Catriona. She sat up and went into her bedside cabinet.

"This calls for a packet of chocolate toffee éclairs," she said. We munched away on the delicious sweets, plotting about how we could find out more about the statue.

"We need to find out if a little girl who loved ballet ever lived here," said Tilda. "Is there anywhere in the castle that might have records about children who used to live here?"

"Yeah, there is somewhere, actually," I said.

"Tell us! Where?" said Catriona.

"It's dead creepy. It's the old nursery at the top of one of the towers," I said. "I once peeked in there with Sorcha, and it seemed really spooky. There's a weird feeling in that room. I thought I saw a ... ghost!"

"Oooh, cool! Let's go up there tomorrow," said Tilda. "There just might be some clues about this statue girl. And we might even see the ghost!" Tilda didn't seem frightened at all.

It made me feel very funny inside to think that I'd seen a real ghost. I didn't tell the girls that it had looked like the statue girl – it all just felt too weird.

"Right, we'll creep up there during morning break," said Catriona.

I went along with the plan reluctantly. What Dad would say if he caught us did not bear thinking about.

Classes began properly the next day. We were to have two hours of "normal" school each morning, and then one hour of ballet before lunch. Straight after lunch, we'd have arts and crafts, then more ballet. After that, there would be supervised prep until the evening meal. Then in the evenings, we could practise ballet if we liked, or just muck around in the sitting room, and generally do our own thing.

Mrs Laidlaw from the village was going to teach us English, geography and history, while Mr Dorkins was the maths and science teacher. Mrs Mathers would teach us cookery and sewing skills. Another part-timer, Miss Morgan, was going to teach us arts and crafts and music.

It was lovely to be taught in such a tiny little class, and we got to know one another very quickly. Despite all our efforts, Leo liked to work alone, so we were still struggling to get to know her.

At break-time, Tilda, Catriona and I went up to the top of the west tower, in search of the old nursery. I was dreading it. Once we were at the top of the tower, I recognised the shabby curtain over the door immediately, and my tummy began to somersault.

"It's behind this curtain, girls," I said. "Who wants to open the door?"

"I'll do it!" said Tilda.

The door creaked as she turned the handle and pushed it open.

"Cool. It's not locked," she said. "Wow! Get a load of this!"

We all followed her into the old nursery. It was just as I remembered it from my first view. I shuddered, feeling that the room was freezing cold, but the others didn't seem to notice. I leaped in the air as something brushed past my left arm. *I'm not imagining it. This room has a presence.*

"What's wrong, Katie?" said Tilda.

"Nothing!" I lied. The other girls hadn't felt anything. Maybe I was just being paranoid.

"This is awesome," said Catriona. "We must find out something about the statue girl in here, surely."

"I'll look in the cupboard," said Tilda. "Cat, you check out that big chest of drawers, and Katie, you look in the toy chest over by the window. If you find anything of interest, anything at all, just yell and we can all check it over. I think we should start a box of secrets for this girl, so we can piece the mystery together."

We all scattered about the room to start researching.

I was paralysed with fear. I looked at the others, setting about their tasks happily. *Come on, Katie,* I said to myself. *Don't be so paranoid.*

I opened the toy chest slowly. The lid was stiff. I managed to get it to rise and as I did so, a hideous toy clown popped up into my face, like a jack-in-the-box.

"Aaarrgh!" I screamed. "It's alive!"

"What's alive?" said Tilda, heading over to investigate.

"This clown!" I said.

"Katie," laughed Catriona. "Calm down. You're crazy. Toy clowns don't come alive. He's been lying in there for years. Stop panicking."

"I'm sorry," I said. "I mean, I'm used to the castle and it's never scared me before, but this nursery just freaks me out; I don't know why."

"Right, I'll do the toy box, and you can do the cupboard," said Tilda. "You've obviously watched Toy Story too many times. Toys don't come to life!"

I went inside the huge cupboard and found an old wooden ladder, which I climbed onto so that I could look at what was on all the shelves.

"I've got something!" called Catriona from the chest of drawers. "The little cardigans here are embroidered with the letters LL, and there are some books with a name inside as well. It says 'Lily Lamont'."

"Keep everything in a pile and we can examine it all carefully down in our room later. Hey, I wonder if Lily's Lake is named after Lily Lamont?" I said.

"Must be," said Tilda. "We need to see if the statue has a plaque with a name on it. Maybe Lily *is* the statue girl. Let's go back to see the statue soon!"

Inside the cupboard, there were bundles of old baby clothes, all very fragile looking, made from lace and old cotton, and there were baby eating things too – silver mugs and china plates, plus cutlery, all engraved with LL. There was a wooden abacus and I saw some jigsaw puzzles too. Then I caught sight of a beautiful jewellery box. It was covered in red velvet cloth and looked as if it was in excellent condition.

I lifted it from the shelf. It was a musical box! The ballerina inside wore a white tutu and her hair was in a bun. I saw a key at the back of the box and turned it. It played the tune from *The Sleeping Beauty*.

"Hey, what's that music?" called Tilda.

"It's a little girl's musical box," I said. "Let's take this down too. I'll put it under my bed."

"Wow!" said Catriona. "Good find."

In the distance, we could hear the bell ringing. "Hey, it's time for ballet class with Willow," said Tilda. "I can't wait."

We hurriedly grabbed our finds and placed them in an old box, then raced down to our bedroom, where we hid the box under my bed.

I think we were supposed to find the statue and investigate this case, I decided. I didn't feel quite so anxious now. And it was fun to be on a secret mission with my new friends.

We ran down to the changing rooms where we put on our ballet stuff. The other girls had already done so, judging by their other school clothes being scattered all over the place.

We trouped into the dance studio. Even though this room had changed so much from the days when it was the ballroom, it still had the same safe and happy feel to it. I was very glad to be here, after the unease I had felt in the old nursery.

16. Divided Loyalties

Willow stood by the barre stretching as we entered the dance studio. There was a lovely piece of music playing softly from Willow's iPod – from the fairies' scene in *Cinderella*.

"I love her leotard!" gasped Eliza, who was always trying out pretty new ballet outfit combos. Willow *did* look stunning. She wore a purple leotard, with a soft pink wraparound skirt. Her tights were purple with white stripes, and her ballet pumps were pale pink. Her hair was up in a soft bun and she wore a white flower at one ear.

"Hi girls!" she said. "I thought we'd just get to know one another today. We'll do some improvisation work, plus cartwheels and exercises. Then as from tomorrow, we can start to put together a routine for the first exhibition for parents. How does that sound?"

We all nodded and smiled happily.

Willow taught us how to let our bodies move in time with music and express emotions through movement rather than words.

By the end of the lesson, we had learned so much.

"She's a brilliant teacher. I've learned more in one lesson with her than I learned in six years with Madame Larch at my old dance school," said Polly.

Everyone agreed. We all loved her. And best of all, she didn't pander to Leo. She treated us equally.

I hardly thought about my family in the first few days of term, as I was busy getting to know all the girls, and getting used to my routine. But most of all, I enjoyed learning from Willow.

"I wish I could dance like Willow," I said one night at teatime in the dining room.

"But, Katie. You probably *will* be that good once you're that age," said Tilda.

"But she's really graceful. I don't think I'll ever be that elegant. And I'll never look that good in practice wear. She's awesome."

Tilda nodded. "I'd like to be a bit skinnier, but, hey, Mrs Mathers' sticky toffee pudding is just too good!" She had polished off two bowlfuls!

"Hey, Leo. What're you having tonight?" called Catriona.

"Tofu and bean tagine," she said. "It's one of the only things that doesn't interfere with my metabolism."

"Poor Mrs Mathers," I muttered. "Imagine having to cook that vile gunk, as well as preparing for us."

Unfortunately Leo heard me.

"It's not my fault that I'm this way," she said.

Just before bedtime that night, Willow came to tell me that my parents wanted to see me down in the flat.

I padded down there in my pyjamas and slippers. I was excited to think that Mum and Dad wanted to see me. "They probably want to apologise for being so mean to me over the last week or so," I thought out loud.

When I got in there, Sorcha and Hamish ran to greet me, showing me paintings and stuff they had made down in Lochvale School, where they were taken each morning by Mrs Renton.

"Hi guys!" I said. "How are you getting on in your new rooms?"

"Good," said Sorcha.

"Not good at all," said Hamish. "I liked my old room much better. The ceiling is way too high in here, and there are monsters in my cupboard."

"Oh really?" I said. "What are these monsters like?"

"They're big and scary and unkind, just like my teacher, Mr Peters," he said.

I laughed. I knew Mr Peters well. He was quite strict and I could imagine that he didn't have much patience with Hamish.

"You two – bedtime," said Dad. "Mum and I need to talk to Katie. We hardly get to see her any more."

"Let me read them a bedtime story each," I said.

When I came back to the kitchen twenty minutes later, Mum and Dad sat at the table, looking quite serious.

"So, how are things going on your side of the school, Katie?" said Mum.

"Cool. Everyone's really nice on the staff. I mean, Willow's just lovely. We all adore her. The other girls are friendly – apart from Leo," I said.

"Yes," said Mum. "Oh, Katie darling – Leo came to see me today and she said that you've been making fun of her food allergies. You know, it's really rather upsetting for her. She can't help having these reactions to certain foods, and she's very embarrassed about it. It would be great if you could try to be a little kinder to her. If you treat her well, then the other girls might follow suit. We don't want to lose such a great talent. And the thing is, darling, we do need quite a few more pupils. Right now, the bill for the staff wages is greater than the fee money we're receiving."

I sat in silence for a few minutes.

"So, what you're saying is that, if I want the Cloudberry School of Ballet to work out, then I have to go along with pandering to Leo?" I said.

"Basically, yes," said Dad. "I know she's difficult, but I'd like you to try a little bit harder to make her feel welcome. Business is tough. We've used almost all of Dr Campbell's book advance money on doing up the castle. And as for the money we received from the sale of the Egyptian artefacts, that's in a special bank account for paying the staff for a year. So, you see, we really do need to make sure that the business makes its own profit, or else it will just flop after the first year or so, and it will be hard to sell it as a dance school, so all the ballet stuff in the studios and whatnot might go to waste. Do you understand how stressful this is for Mum and me?"

"Yes, I understand," I said. "I'll see what I can do with Leo. But she's just impossible to like."

"Do your best, darling," said Mum. "We'll get through this teething stage and then we'll all relax and start to have fun."

As far as I was concerned, I'd never have fun again while Leo was around.

When we started dancing properly with Willow each day, we began to see what an amazing dancer Leo was.

"I hate to say it, girls," I said one day as we stood in a line to do a *jeté* across the studio, "but she has a very special talent. There's something so likeable about her when she dances that you don't get to see the rest of the time."

"Yeah, I s'pose so," agreed Tilda. "But it doesn't make up for what she's like the rest of the time."

"Why don't we try to be nice to her?" I suggested, thinking about what Mum and Dad had asked me to do.

"Are you crazy? She doesn't deserve it. When has she ever done something nice for us?" said Catriona.

"I know, I know. Well, I'm going to give it a try. I'll ask her if she'd like to play some games with us in the sitting room tonight and see how it goes," I said.

"Fair enough. Your choice," said Catriona.

Leo was limbering up at the barre, waiting for her turn to jump.

"Hey, Leo," I said. "Would you like to play some board games and stuff with us in the sitting room tonight. It'll be a laugh," I said.

"No thanks," she replied. "I'm not very good at games like that."

"But we can teach you. And anyway, it's just a bit of fun," I said.

"But I don't do fun. I have to be the best at everything. My mother expects it," she said, rather sadly.

I felt a little bit sorry for her, but I knew that when I told the others she had refused to join us, they would hate her even more.

"Well, if you change your mind, let me know," I said.

17. Poor Bella

Towards the end of each ballet lesson, Willow always left a little bit of time for chatting. We would gather round her in a circle. It was just like having a big sister – something I had always wanted.

"What's it like to be part of the Scottish Ballet?" I asked.

"Hard work," she replied. "But such fun. It makes you so proud to belong to a proper ballet troupe. You all muck in together, and it's so exciting to go on tour. But always, the quality of the ballet comes first. We practise for hours every day. There's no slacking off. It's just essential to keep your skills polished."

"What was it like when you auditioned with them?" asked Catriona.

"Gosh, I was so nervous, but I just forgot that they were watching me. You have to connect with your ballet, and let the energy take over."

We all listened with awe as Willow talked about her life with the Scottish Ballet.

"Now girls, let's finish by doing some limbering. Let me see you all at the barre doing stretches," she said.

When the bell for lunch rang, we all wanted to go outside as it was sunny and warm, even though there was a smoky autumnal smell in the air.

"I'm going to give you girls a picnic lunch today," said Mrs Mathers. "I'll spread it out on the picnic benches by the cedar tree. I'll be there in five minutes, but if any of you would like to help me, that would be much appreciated."

We all went into the kitchen and helped Mrs Mathers place the lunch things in baskets and boxes – all except Leo. She had made her way over to the stable block to check on The Duke.

We enjoyed a lovely egg and ham pie, and salady things, all washed down with homemade cloudy lemonade, plus a late summer fruit fool afterwards – which was super-scrummy.

"I think I'll go and check on little Bella now," I said. "Anyone want to come?"

"Yes, me!" said all of the girls at once, so off we trotted over to the stables.

When we got in there, we saw that Leo was standing in Bella's old stable, brushing down The Duke with a dandy brush. But there was another change. I stood gaping in disbelief.

I knew that The Duke was now in Bella's stable – but Leo had also put all of his things in the next biggest stable, which should have been Bella's new one. There were at least three amazing saddles, loads of bridles, halters, blankets, grooming kit and numnahs galore. So where had she put poor little Bella?

"Where's Bella?" I said.

"Don't worry, she's perfectly happy in the end stall," said Leo breezily.

"The end stall?" I said. "That's not a stall. It's a cupboard! She's far too big for that!"

I couldn't believe that she'd moved Bella once again, into a tiny little half-stable on the end, which was not much bigger than a large dog kennel.

"Leo! How dare you move my pony without asking?" I said.

"But I *did* ask," said Leo. "Your mum said I could."

"I can't believe that," I said.

I refused to believe that Mum would have done this. I took Bella out of the stable block and led her out to the picnic benches, where I tethered her to a fence.

"We'll sort this out later, Bella," I said.

18. Secret Plan

That afternoon, Mum took us for a ballet class about the Big Show, which she was in charge of producing.

"Girls, as you would expect, we want to put on a wonderful show for your parents this Christmas – a show which will display all our talents here at Cloudberry Castle.

I have decided that we will perform *The Sleeping Beauty*, a gorgeous ballet, with many delightful roles within it. I will soon be holding auditions for the main roles, and from what I know of your talents, I will have a very hard choice to make. You would all be wonderful as Princess Aurora, but of course I can pick only one."

For some reason, all eyes in the room turned to Leo, as if we just knew that there was no point even trying when she was around.

Mum played the score of the ballet and demonstrated some of the roles.

"Girls, sit down and watch carefully," she said. "These are the dances which will feature in the Big Show."

I was so proud of her – she's still the finest dancer I've ever seen, even better than Willow, if I'm honest.

As Mum glided round the studio, executing lovely *pirouettes, fouettés* and a magnificent *grand jeté*, Leo began to join in, dancing alongside Mum.

She danced beautifully. But why, oh why, could she not do as she was told, like the rest of us?

After the lesson, there was a break for afternoon tea, which is when Mrs Mathers spoils us in the drawing room – with teeny sandwiches, freshly baked warm scones, spread with creamy butter and cloudberry jam, flapjacks and fresh fruit juice or milkshakes.

At the end of afternoon tea, Mum came into the room to see me.

"I heard some of the girls talking about the situation with Bella, and I've got a perfect solution!" said Mum. "Bella is going to move into the castle courtyard, where there's a gorgeous stable just the right size for her, so that means she'll be even closer to you and you can check on her much more easily. Isn't that perfect?"

"That's great Mum, thanks," I said.

Mum went off with a big smile on her face.

"You know what that means, don't you?" said Tilda.

"What?" I said.

"She's not actually dealing with Leo; she's just making her ego even bigger by letting Leo win every time."

"I guess you're right, but what can I do?" I said.

"I dunno. There has to be something," said Tilda.

"Yeah ... why don't we practise extra hard for the auditions?" I said. "Then we might beat her to the main roles. We've got to fight this takeover!"

"Too right!" said Tilda. "We'll go to the studio whenever we can. We'll show her she's not the only one who can dance."

That night, after lights out, we found our torches and went through Lily Lamont's things.

Tilda began scanning all the papers in the box.

"Look at this," she said. "It's a 'Get Well' card to Lily, from her mother. It has ballet shoes on the front, and it says, 'Keep dancing, darling!' inside."

"So she could be the statue girl," said Catriona.

"You wouldn't put up a statue of a child unless they died, would you?" I said, thinking aloud.

"And maybe she died of whatever was wrong with her when she got this card?" suggested Tilda.

I stared straight ahead, deep in thought.

"You're so quiet, Katie. What's wrong?" asked Catriona.

"Oh, nothing," I said.

"Come on, there's something, isn't there?" pressed Tilda.

"Okay then. When I was in the old nursery, I saw an apparition of a girl in an old-fashioned ballet outfit," I confessed. "She looked just like the statue. But I hadn't seen the statue when I first saw her."

"No way! Cool!" said Tilda. "I want to see her too! We have to go back to the island and find out what's written on the statue."

I shuddered. I hated to think about what might have happened to lovely little Lily.

In ballet class the next day, during our last five minutes, Tilda, Catriona and I chatted about the ballerina statue.

"Let's go over to see the statue tonight after dark," said Tilda.

"Yeah," agreed Catriona. "I want to solve the mystery. I mean, is it Lily? And what happened to her?"

Willow hovered around us as we spoke.

"Everything okay, girls?" she said.

"Yeah, sure," I said. "Just chatting."

"That's good. Because you wouldn't want to break any school rules, would you?" she said.

"No, of course not." Tilda smiled sweetly.

After class, we confirmed the plan.

"So, we'll need torches, warm clothes and flat shoes," I said. "And I promise you – this is the last time that I'm going against Mum's rules."

19. Lily's Lake

Tilda and I did an hour of extra ballet work in the studio after tea; we were determined to shine at the auditions. We were very hyper, thinking about the island, so our obsessive revision of our *pas de cheval* steps kept us occupied.

I knew that Mum and Dad would be furious if they found out about the island. But they hardly seemed to have time for me any more – they only seemed to care about the business – so I felt it didn't matter what they thought.

Willow came round to tell us to put lights out, and we all snuggled under our duvets as though it was any old night. When she had gone into her room, we got up and pulled sweaters over our nighties, with jeans under them, along with trainers, hats and scarves.

We sneaked downstairs and out into the night.

We tiptoed over to the bridge, with Tilda at the front.

"This bridge is so flimsy," said Tilda. "Let me go first, then one of you at a time," she said.

When we got on to the island, we all shone our torches to see the way ahead. The heavy foliage was overhanging, and it dangled onto our faces.

"Arrrrggghhhh!" screamed Catriona. "This is way too creepy. I want to turn back!"

"It's fine," said Tilda. "It's just your imagination playing tricks on you, that's all."

But when we neared the statue, we all stood transfixed looking at little Lily, through the weeds that surrounded her.

"Did you see her move?" I breathed.

"I'm not sure," said Tilda. "I thought I saw her arm move. But that's silly."

"She *did* move!" insisted Catriona.

"Oh no!" I said. "Let's get out of here. Statues shouldn't move!"

"Calm down," said Tilda. "I want to see if there's a plaque on it. We've come all this way."

We approached the statue nervously.

"I can't see anything written," I said, shining my torch at the statue.

"Let's push back this ivy," said Tilda, certain that we'd find something.

We pulled at the gripping ivy, which seemed determined to hide the statue's secrets.

"Look!" I said. "Here's a little plaque at the bottom of the plinth."

Tilda took out a notebook and scribbled as she read aloud, "Our little ballerina, Lady Lily Lamont, taken from us too soon. Dancing in heaven. 1921."

"Oooh, spooky. She did die. How sad," said Catriona.

We all started to run back to the bridge.

"You girls go over first," said Tilda. "Quickly, get to the other side!"

Catriona crossed first as she was so terrified. Then I went across. Next came Tilda.

She leapt across it with such speed that she caught her foot in one of the wooden slats as she went. *Splat!* She fell flat on her face.

"Ouch! My ankle!" she cried. "It's twisted."

"Can you get up?" asked Catriona.

"No, I don't think so. I'm in agony!" said Tilda.

"We'll have to carry her up to the room," I said.

"Yes, good idea," said Catriona.

As we tried to help Tilda, we heard footsteps approaching.

"Oh no! What if it's my dad?" I said.

"Sssh, keep quiet," said Catriona.

There was definitely someone nearing us.

It was Willow!

"Girls, what's going on?" she said.

"Sorry, we were just exploring, and Tilda's had an accident," I explained.

"I was afraid you were planning something silly like this when I heard you chatting in class today, but I couldn't be sure. I thought I'd better come out to check on you, and I'm glad I did!" she said.

"Oh, Willow, *please* don't tell my parents what we've done," I said. "I don't want them to know that I've let them down yet again. We can say Tilda has a ballet injury – please. We'll never do anything this silly again."

"Well, I'll sleep on it," said Willow. "And I'll let you know what I decide to do at ballet class tomorrow. But in the meantime, let's see if we can find a bandage for poor Tilda's ankle."

We carried Tilda awkwardly upstairs. She did so much moaning and complaining, I'm surprised we didn't wake the ancestors in the portraits, never mind my mum and dad. We got her clothes off so she was just in her nightie and we laid her on her bed, then we took off our outdoor stuff too. Willow went to fetch a bandage from the first-aid kit in reception. She came back quickly and strapped up Tilda's ankle, and gave her two painkillers.

"Goodnight, girls," said Willow. "You've been very naughty disobeying the rules. It was dangerous to cross that bridge; you're lucky that no one was seriously hurt. I want you to promise you'll never sneak out again."

"We promise, Willow," we all said together.

"Now get some sleep. See you at class tomorrow."

"Night night, Willow," we said, and promptly fell asleep.

20. Bad Dreams

I woke in the night. I had a crazy, colourful dream, with swirling images of Cloudberry Castle, Lily's Lake, the ballerina statue and Dr Campbell.

I sensed a presence at the bottom of my bed again. I opened my eyes. There she was! It was Lily, in her ballet outfit, with a pale, poorly face and those haunted, tormented eyes.

"Lily, what's wrong?" I said softly.

I got out of bed, and as I did so, she seemed to move towards me.

My breathing was fast and my heart thumped.

Lily vanished before me.

"Lily!" I called softly.

All I could think of was having a big hug from Mum. I ran out of the room and down to our family flat.

I crept along to my parents' room.

"Mum," I whispered. "I need to talk to you."

"What's wrong, Katie?" she asked. "What's happened?"

"Mum, I've had a nightmare," I said.

She got up.

"I'll make some warm milk," she said, and we went along to the kitchen, where she made the comforting drink, plus some toast with Holly Cottage raspberry jam.

"Tell me what's troubling you," she said. "I've never known you to have nightmares."

So, I told her everything – about our trips to the island, the presence in the old nursery, and the ghostly apparitions of Lily Lamont at the bottom of my bed.

"Katie, you know you shouldn't go on that bridge," said Mum. "It's dangerous."

"I know, I'm sorry. It was lucky that Willow heard us, and she helped us to get Tilda up to bed," I said.

"Wait a minute. Willow knows you went over to the island?" said Mum.

"Well, she only just found out by accident," I said.

"But why didn't she come to talk to Dad and I as soon as she knew? She cannot keep secrets from us. What will Tilda's parents say when they hear about her accident?" said Mum.

"But we begged Willow not to tell you," said Katie.

"This gets worse. I'll sort this out tomorrow. You go into your own bed down here for now. And I'll talk to Willow in the morning," said Mum. "And as for ghosts? Katie, they're nothing more than a figment of your imagination. It sounds like you girls have been a little over-imaginative lately. However, the story of Lily Lamont and her love of ballet sounds fascinating, especially for the ballet school, I will admit."

I crept up to my other bed at sunrise, but the truth was out now. *I hope I haven't got Willow into trouble,* I thought.

Mum took another Big Show ballet class that day, so we didn't actually see Willow for our ballet lesson.

"I wonder what Willow's planning to do?" said Catriona. "Do you think she'll tell your parents about the island trip?"

"I don't think it matters now. I had a nightmare and I ended up telling Mum everything," I admitted.

"Katie!" said Catriona. "That was daft!"

"I know," I said. "But I do daft things in the middle of the night."

"I'd hate to be you, with your parents running the school. What I love about it here is the fact that my parents aren't around to see what I get up to," said Catriona.

"Yeah, at first I thought it was a great thing having

them here," I said. "But now, I'm starting to wonder as well."

"Girls, we're heading along to the costume room today," said Mum. "We can see what outfits will be suitable for *The Sleeping Beauty*, and what sort of headdresses we might need. Don't forget, we can adapt items to better suit our production. Gaining a feel for sewing and costume design is all part of becoming a great ballerina. Let's go dress up!"

"Yeah!" squealed all the girls, and even Leo looked excited. I felt so sorry for Tilda, stuck up in the bedroom with her sore ankle. She would have loved to dress up!

Mum didn't look as if she was angry about anything. *I hope she's forgiven Willow for last night!* I thought.

"Madam Mackenzie, what are the main parts in *The Sleeping Beauty*?" asked Polly.

"Well, there's obviously the role of Princess Aurora herself. But there are some other delightful parts too. For example, there's Candide, and Fleur de Farine. Oh and there's Canari qui Chante. Not to forget the Gold, Silver, Sapphire and Diamond Fairies. What could be prettier than dressing all these fairies? And Katie and I ordered some wonderful new costumes especially for this show. So come on, let's have some fun!" said Mum.

We all galloped along to the "dress-up" room. Mum and Dad had fitted some mirrors with lights around the edges, and the shelves were filled with the shoes, feather headdresses and other pretty accessories we had ordered. I knew this was why I'd hardly seen anything of my parents; they'd been so busy putting everything together for the girls arriving.

"Hey, Katie!" said Catriona. "You sit at this mirror and I'll put your hair up!"

"Why don't I show you all how to do the perfect ballet bun?" suggested Mum.

"Cool!" we all cried.

Mum chose Polly to be her model as she has hair that's very suitable for a perfect bun.

We were all transfixed as Mum expertly pinned Polly's hair into a lovely high bun.

"And now for the fun part," said Mum. "Let's add a tiara and some flowers."

We were all engrossed, admiring Polly.

Then Eliza called out, "Hey! Look at Leo...".

21. Willow's Disgrace

Leo had changed into the full outfit for Princess Aurora! The tutu was divine. It was white satin, embroidered with pretty patterns, and stitched with sequins. The skirt didn't hang down in folds; it went straight out in a stiff skirt, with layers of firm tulle and it was decorated with beads and pearls. It was quite simply the most wonderful tutu any of us had ever seen. The tiara that went with it was also very beautiful, high and dazzling with sparkling teardrops.

Leo *was* Princess Aurora.

"This seems to fit me perfectly," she declared, doing a little twirl.

We all looked aghast and turned to Mum. No one had said we could try on tutus.

Mum looked distressed.

"But Leo," she said. "we have yet to choose the parts

for the show. And I did not say that you could try that on, did I?"

"Oh, Mrs Mackenzie!" said Leo suddenly, stumbling and grabbing her throat. "I think I must have been allergic to something at breakfast! Help me! I'm choking!"

Mum ran over to her. I wasn't sure if the choking fit was real or not, but it did look very convincing.

"Katie, get her inhaler!" said Mum. She laid Leo out on the floor and held her hand while everyone waited.

I found the inhaler in Leo's room and rushed back. Mum gave her some puffs from it and Leo sat up.

She looked very weak and woozy.

"So *can* I be Princess Aurora?" she asked, in a pathetic little voice.

As Catriona and I went for lunch that day, we saw Willow slipping into Mum's office behind reception.

"Oh no!" said Catriona. "Your mum must have sent for her. Let's listen in."

We snooped up to the door. At first we couldn't hear anything.

But then we heard Mum.

"I have never allowed my children over that bridge.

Dr Campbell always said it wasn't safe," she said.

"I'm so terribly sorry. I wanted to let you know what they'd done, and I'm sure I would have. But I hated to betray the girls. Please give me another chance, Mrs Mackenzie. I love it here," said Willow, between sobs.

"How can we trust you to put the girls' best interests first? I'll have to think this over, Willow. I am very disappointed in you. In the meantime, I'll have to suspend you from teaching. I'll call an agency for a supply teacher while we sort this out."

"Oh no!" said Catriona.

A taxi arrived for Willow soon after lunch. We all watched from the art room window as she got inside, and it drove off down the long driveway and out of the Cloudberry estate.

"Will we ever see her again?" sobbed Polly.

"Who knows?" I said.

"Do we have another ballet teacher yet?" I asked Mum later that day.

"Yes. A Madame Fussette is arriving in the morning. Katie, I can't believe you went out after dark. This just isn't going to work out unless we all stick to some rules around here. I cannot run the risk of something awful happening to a girl in our care. Look at Tilda's injury – that will heal – but what if she'd drowned in the lake?"

"Mum, I'm so sorry. But Willow only heard us after the event – she didn't encourage us to do it. She doesn't have much teaching experience, but she's a brilliant teacher. I so want her to stay. We all do."

"Katie, I'll have to consider this carefully and it's not fair on Willow to have her stay here while I do that. Let's leave the subject for now. I'm very busy," said Mum.

Tilda and I did extra ballet practice again that night. We were driven to dance as well as our beloved Willow – to show how well she'd taught us – so we perfected our *brisés, échappés* and *pas de basques*.

22. TV Showdown

Madame Fussette was waiting for us in the studio the next day.

"She's at least ninety!" said Eliza.

"Try a hundred!" said Polly.

"Girls, I'd like to see you dance in pairs. Perhaps we'll do a *battement fondu*, followed by a *développé*, then a *sauté*, and finally, an *enchainement* of your choice," said Madame Fussette.

I was paired with Leo. We practised our little routine, but when the music started, Leo followed a different plan.

"I thought we agreed to dance as a team," I hissed.

"Well, if you could only keep time," spat Leo.

When we finished, Madame Fussette clasped her hands together excitedly.

"Leo, how lovely! Exquisite steps! What a talent. Delightful," she said.

It was as if I didn't exist.

I definitely must practise even more, I decided. The way things were going I'd never get to dance the lead role in *The Sleeping Beauty.*

But the praise for Leo turned us all against the elderly new ballet teacher. Madame Fussette could do nothing right as far as we were concerned, as we pined for our Willow.

The days went by and we didn't forget Willow, but we learned to live without her. But Madame Fussette became more and more admiring of Leo McLennan.

"Bravo, Leo!" she cried.

"Girls, watch how Leo does it!"

"Ah, Leo. A lovely interpretation!"

It seemed as if things couldn't get any worse with Leo. She simply could not think about anyone but herself, she still refused to join in when we played games, and none of us enjoyed her company.

One morning in the autumn term, a TV crew arrived at the reception of Cloudberry, with loads of cameras, microphones and sound stuff. Tilda and I were coming out of the dining room from breakfast. Mum appeared. She looked very glamorous, all dressed up in one of her lovely floral dresses, with black patent pumps. Her hair was nicely blow-dried and fell softly over her face, which was glowing with some pretty make-up.

"Ah, you must be from the *Little Ballerina* reality TV show?" she said. "I presume you're here to film a piece all about our little star, Leo McLennan?"

"Yeah, I'm Paul Davies, the producer. We've heard from her mother that she's really quite a dancer. So, we'll be here for three days, if that's okay?" said Paul.

"That's fine. And when will the programme go out on air?" asked Mum.

"In a couple of months – prime time. Ballet is huge right now," he said.

"Great," said Mum. "Just ask if you need anything. Johnny will show you up to your rooms."

Tilda couldn't believe her ears.

"Your mum is crazy! This is just going to make Leo's ego even bigger!" she said.

"I don't know what's going on," I admitted. "There must be some reason why Mum had agreed to this."

★ ✦ ✦ ✶ ✴

That afternoon, we were dancing in the studio, when the film crew barged in, disrupting the flow of our lesson.

Paul the producer chatted to Madame Fussette.

"Girls," she called. "Everyone except Leo must sit

down. Leo is to be filmed dancing solo. Come along, Leo. This will be a treat for us all."

"Can you direct me, Madame?" said Leo nervously. "My mother will be furious if I'm less than perfect."

The TV crew were so annoying. Everywhere we turned, the cameramen were there, catching us off-guard, and asking personal questions. Mum had told me they weren't supposed to talk to us at all.

"Ugh!" said Catriona. "I can't bear this. How come Leo gets to be on telly?"

"Her mum has probably paid them to have her on the show," said Eliza.

"I actually think she's a bit scared of her mum," I said, thinking of Leo's comment in the studio.

After breakfast on the second morning, the TV guys approached Tilda and I as we went to history class.

"Hey, girls. Got a minute?" said Paul, walking us over to a quiet corner.

"What is it?" I said.

"This Leo is unreal. She's going to be a great TV villain. We think the viewers will love to hate her. D'you young ladies want to say a piece to camera about what it's like being at school with such a prima donna?" said Paul.

Tilda's eyes lit up.

I was nervous. *Just think of the harm it could do to Cloudberry,* I thought. And no matter how sick I was of

Leo, it didn't seem right to say mean things about her on telly.

"There's no way we could do that," I said.

"Right," said Paul. "I understand. But here's another idea. How about you secretly help us make Leo look like even more of a diva than she is!"

"What would we have to do?" asked Tilda, eyes glistening.

"Well, we could discuss it at break," said Paul. "I have a few ideas."

"Okay, I'd like to hear them," said Tilda.

"Well, I'm having nothing to do with it," I said, walking away from them.

23. Leo Disappears

For the next couple of days, nothing went right for Leo. Her best ballet clothes mysteriously disappeared, and she was caught on camera moaning about it. Then she slipped on the studio floor during a special dance for the TV show – the floor had been somehow "over-polished".

"Who did this?" she yelled. "My mother will punish you!"

Again, the cameras caught her hissy fit.

On another occasion, her special food was "accidentally" knocked to the ground.

"Aaargh!" she wailed. "What will I eat? I'm allergic to absolutely everything else!"

Every time things went wrong for Leo, Tilda and Eliza were never far away.

On the final day of filming, the whole ballet school was meant to do a dance around Leo, who was going to take on the role of the principal ballerina, centre stage. I had heard the girls muttering about it up in the sitting room, but I didn't get involved.

When it was time to perform the dance, all the other girls pulled cheeky faces to the camera, and did a silly dance, just to spoil Leo's moment of glory.

"I hate you all!" screamed Leo. "You're jealous!"

I saw the producer give a thumbs-up to Tilda, as Leo stormed off.

She was in floods of tears. I went after her. I felt that things were getting too crazy now. She didn't deserve this.

But Leo had run out of the front door of Cloudberry and into the estate. By the time I got out, there was no sign of her.

I ran back inside. "Leo's gone missing! She's run away!" I called.

The TV crew came running out with their cameras. Mrs Mathers hurried out in her apron. Mum and Dad were just behind her, and Johnny joined us. Miss Morgan got involved. Madame Fussette appeared. And the other girls followed. We all started charging around the grounds calling out for Leo.

"Check the stables!" said Mum.

But she wasn't with The Duke.

We were concerned. What if she ran all the way up to the main road? Or maybe she was so sad and angry she might slip and fall in the lake? The estate was so huge, we didn't know how we'd ever find her.

Dad called us all together.

"We'd better do this systematically," he said. He split us into groups and gave us instructions to head off in various directions.

"And as for you guys!" he said, turning to the TV crew. "You can switch off those blinking cameras, and while we're at it, let me tell you that I'm withdrawing our permission for you to use footage from your filming here. There has been nothing but chaos since you got here. If I didn't know better, I'd say you've been baiting Leo to make her act even brattier than usual. Well done guys! A little girl has gone missing now!"

The TV crew looked very ashamed of themselves, and they laid down their kit and joined the search. Some of us were on foot, others on bicycles. A few were in cars, and there was even one quad bike, which Dad had recently bought. He jumped on it and screeched off.

Tilda, Catriona and I were part of the same search team. We seemed to be out there for ages. Most of us had phones and were supposed to call each other with news. But no calls came through.

"Oh, I'm so worried," said Tilda. "What if something awful happens to her? And it's all my fault!"

"She'll be fine. She's just hiding," I said, trying to convince myself. "But the TV guys had no right to mix us up in their nasty take on Leo. We're kids. It's terrible to treat us that way."

"You're right. What was I thinking? I didn't mean to be cruel. I didn't think she had any feelings to hurt," said Tilda.

"Everyone has feelings," I said.

We wandered about, calling out for Leo, but the whole estate seemed eerily quiet.

"What if she disappears for ever and ever, and we never find out what happened to her?" said Catriona.

"That's not a helpful thought," I said. "We have to stay positive."

"Look!" cried Tilda, kicking up a pile of leaves. "Here's a shoe!"

We gathered round. "That's one of my old shoes," I said. "I wondered what had happened to that!"

Every rustle of leaves or patter of footprints gave us a flutter of hopeful excitement.

"We really want to find her, don't we?" said Tilda. "D'you think that means we like her now?"

"Yeah. I think we must," I said.

24. Changes

We all went quiet after that, using all our energy to look out for clues.

After what seemed like an eternity, my phone rang.

It was Dad.

"We've got her," he said. "She was almost at Tullyacre Farm. She's sobbing so much she's going to wear herself out. Come back to the castle."

"Okay Dad. I'll call some of the others," I said.

The strangest thing happened when we saw Leo shuddering in a blanket in the drawing room. We all ran over to hug her. At first, her body was rigid and tense. But eventually she relaxed and hugged us back.

"Why did you all look for me?" she asked.

"Because we were worried about you," said Tilda.

"Really? Why would you care about me?" said Leo.

"Cos you're one of us," said Tilda.

"Are you kidding me?" said Leo.

"No, I'm serious. I'm sorry, Leo," said Tilda.

"Me too," said Eliza.

Everyone apologised for the way she had been treated.

"It's my own fault," said Leo. "I don't know how to be friends with anyone. I've never had a friend."

"Well, we can teach you," I said.

No one noticed when the TV crew drove away from Cloudberry.

Our problems seemed smaller from that day, and life at Cloudberry Castle School of Ballet became great fun. The only sadness was that Mum and Dad decided it was too soon to welcome Willow back, and we were stuck with Madame Fussette.

Leo improved a lot – she joined in with games in the sitting room and didn't practise all the time. She was still odd, but we mostly accepted her oddities.

It was very sad and lonely when everyone got picked up for the mid-term break in October.

We all hugged each for ages in the reception area.

"Text me!" said Tilda.

"And me!" said Leo. "I'll give you all my number!"

We were shocked! She had never offered us her phone number before. It was a breakthrough moment.

Mum and Dad tried to be all "family time" over the holiday, but I had changed so much, it didn't feel the same any more.

I spent every day in the studio practising dance routines for the *Sleeping Beauty* auditions. My *glissé* wasn't quite right and I tried it a hundred times.

One day, Mum asked me to look after Hamish and Sorcha while she and Dad went for a walk in the grounds.

"Come on, you two," I said. "You can give me marks out of ten for my dance steps in the studio."

"Yay!" said Hamish. "It'll be like a talent show! I'll be the mean judge, because I hate ballet."

"Okay, you can be the meany," I laughed.

When I put on the music and began to travel across the studio floor as the Gold Fairy, doing continuous *pas de chat*, Hamish was actually quite gripped. He and Sorcha made scorecards.

"How was I then?" I asked.

Sorcha held up a 10 while Hamish held up a 0.

"You cheeky little monkey!" I said, chasing him round the studio.

Everyone was due back the day before Halloween. Johnny, Mrs Mathers and I decorated the castle as a surprise for the girls. It turned out to be Johnny's favourite time of the year. There were spiders' webs, bats and witches' brooms plus all kinds of monster faces all the way up the stairway. Johnny filled boxes with monster brains (jelly and melon seeds) and witches' eyeballs (grapes in cold custard). He invented games which involved walking through a dark hallway hung with tickly cobwebs, and another all about making a witches' potion. Mrs Mathers made special food: worms – spaghetti mud – crumbly chocolate sponge; engine oil – runny chocolate sauce; and frog jelly – lime jelly with gummy sweets through it.

25. Halloween

The girls all arrived back one by one.

It took ages for everyone to say hello to each other, unpack and generally settle down again.

"Hey, I love the castle!" said Tilda.

"So spooky," said Catriona. "Cool! All the ghosts will come out!"

I hope not! I thought.

Finally, it fell dark on Halloween.

"Time to dress up!" I said. "My mum says we can use the costume room with the big mirrors."

We wore witches' cloaks and hats, and painted our faces with hideous white make-up, adding green and black lipstick and eye shadow. I was pretty much creeped out before the activities even began.

"Anyone care to feel some witches' eyeballs?" asked Johnny.

"No thanks," I said. But the other girls loved it and screamed when they touched the "eyeballs".

As the night went on, Catriona, Tilda and I started to dare each other to visit the old nursery.

"There's no way I'm going in there," I said.

"I'm going!" said Tilda.

Trust Tilda!

We all trouped up to the top of the tower and Tilda pulled back the curtain and opened the door.

"Tell me if the chair's rocking," I said.

"Oh yeah, it's going back and forward, and there's an old witch sitting in it!" laughed Tilda. "Seriously, stop being daft."

She persuaded us all to go into the room. A chill wind rushed over me as I entered and I felt as though I was being watched. But I still wanted to find out more about Lily.

"Well, as we're in here," I said, "we may as well do some detective work. Let's see if we can find out what happened to Lily."

A deathly hush fell over the old nursery as we all very carefully carried on with our search from last time.

I shuddered as we examined more of the dusty old things, which had belonged to Lily Lamont. Then I heard a faint noise, and I froze.

"Mama. Help me, Mama," said a child's voice.

Was it Lily? I looked around. No one else seemed to hear it. *I've just got an over-active imagination; that's what Mum said*, I thought.

"I'm freezing, Mama," said the same voice. Then I heard a childish cry. "Don't let me die, Mama."

Silence again.

"I think we found everything the last time," I said, itching to get out of the room now.

"Don't give up," said Tilda.

Then the little girl appeared before me, in her ballet clothes as before. Her image was clear now, as though she was as real as Tilda or Catriona.

She beckoned me over, floating to the other end of the nursery, while I followed.

She stopped and pointed to a panel in the wall.

I recalled Dr Campbell's secret cupboard in the library and pressed the panel.

"What are you doing, Katie?" asked Tilda.

"There's something in here," I said.

I peered into the space in the wall and reached in for some papers.

"What is it?" asked Catriona.

"It's a newspaper clipping from September 1921. The heading is: "Lady Lily Lamont loses fight for life," I said.

"What does the article say?" Tilda asked, moving over to see the newspaper.

I read from it:

> Little Lady Lily Lamont, from Cloudberry
> Castle, Lochvale, Perthshire, perished yesterday,
> when she failed to recover from a chill caught
> on the family's lake within the estate. She died
> in her nurse's arms in the castle's nursery. Her
> distraught parents said: "We will never cope
> without our little dancer. Lily danced through
> the corridors of Cloudberry in her favourite
> ballet shoes and that is how we will always
> remember her."

"Oh, how sad!" Tilda gasped. "We guessed she must
have died young, but now that we've seen her music box
and her cardigans, and her dolls, it seems so tragic."

"I know. Poor little Lily," sniffed Catriona.

"Here's a photograph of her," I said. Of course, I'd
seen her several times before.

We gathered round to look at our little friend, Lily
Lamont.

She was very dainty, dressed in the familiar ballet dress
and her favourite ballet shoes.

"I think we should have this photograph enlarged and
hung up in the hallway of the castle," I decided.

"That's a lovely idea," said Tilda.

I wiped a few tears from my eyes. But the strange thing was that the old nursery didn't seem creepy any more. The chill and the eeriness had disappeared. And so had the vision of Lily Lamont.

26. The Auditions

As soon as Halloween was over, it was time to hold auditions for the Christmas show – *The Sleeping Beauty*. It seemed as if everyone thought the role of Princess Aurora was already in the bag. We just knew it would go to Leo. But we didn't give up hope. Tilda and I still went to the studio after tea every night, and we danced and danced, trying to perfect the steps for Princess Aurora in my case, and The Lilac Fairy in Tilda's case.

"I know I'll never be the princess," I said during one of our attempts at a *grand battement en cloche*. "But I just want to feel that I gave it my all."

"Yeah, I've got to admit that Leo would be lovely as Princess Aurora," said Tilda. "But you're just as good a dancer."

"Thanks," I said, stretching my leg on the barre, and dipping into a *demi-plié*.

"What a term we've had," said Tilda.

"Yeah, I know. But this show is really special. The first show with the first Cloudberry girls. Apparently, there's a whole new batch coming after Christmas. It will never be the same here again," I said.

"Yeah, it'll change. But we'll be the old-timers who can show the new girls what to do," said Tilda.

"I just wish we hadn't lost Willow. She was magical," I said.

"Yeah. But I guess she was in the wrong by not telling your parents straight away," said Tilda.

"But we all make mistakes," I said.

"I would certainly agree with that!" laughed Tilda. "I'm the worst."

When we got up to the sitting room, there was a great commotion going on.

"*Little Ballerina* reality show is on. And they're showing the stuff at Cloudberry!" said Millie. "C'mon, you're missing it."

We were all glued to the screen.

"Mum and Dad will go crazy!" I said. "They didn't want it shown."

Leo sat on one of the sofas with her head in her hands. I put my arm around her.

"Come on, just laugh about it," I said.

"But I was terrible! Moaning and having tantrums the whole time," she said.

As we watched the show, we realised that they had only included good bits about Cloudberry and Leo.

"The castle looks lovely!" said Polly.

"If I didn't come to school here, I would want to come," said Eliza.

"And Leo, you seem really sweet in it," said Tilda. "It's amazing what editing can do!"

We all laughed.

I ran down to the family flat to let them know it was on.

Mum and Dad switched on the TV. At first, they were furious, but as the show went on, and Cloudberry came over so well, they began to smile. Maybe Paul the producer had an attack of guilt! They certainly didn't show any of the hissy fits.

The next day, the school telephone rang off the hook. Every ballerina in the country wanted to come to Cloudberry Castle School of Ballet.

"Looks like we'll have to open a waiting list," said Dad from behind the reception desk. "Things are looking up!"

The day of the auditions arrived. As we went into the ballroom studio, we did a double take.

Willow was back!

Mum's face was beaming with smiles.

"A little surprise for my girls. We could not put on *The Sleeping Beauty* without an expert from the Scottish Ballet, could we now?" she said.

We all ran over to hug Willow.

"It's lovely to have you back," I said.

"And it's great to be back. From now on, I'll be doing what's right for the school," she said.

We had our beloved Willow back.

"Madame Fussette is staying on too," said Mum. "But Willow is going to hold a practice class before the auditions."

We followed Willow around the studio as she demonstrated an *échappé* and a *hortensia*.

Leo was as determined to impress Willow as I was. As we travelled round the studio, Leo got closer and closer to me.

"Are you trying to trip me up?" I asked, with a grin.

"*Moi?*" Leo smiled.

Okay, so she'd improved, but no one changes completely!

It was time for the auditions. We sat on benches in the corridor, waiting to be called into the studio. Mum, Willow and Madame Fussette sat at a table, and they played a piece from *The Sleeping Beauty* for each dancer.

We peered through a glass panel to the side of the door as each girl danced as though her life depended on it.

I was third to go, after Polly and Allie. I danced as perfectly as I could. And Leo looked amazing, as always. But we're all lovely dancers – that's why we're at ballet school.

When Mum, Madame Fussette and Willow finally decided who would dance Princess Aurora, we all got a shock.

"The part of Princess Aurora," said Mum, "goes to Polly! You all danced beautifully, girls, but the maturity and excellent behaviour Polly has displayed throughout the term made her stand out. We know we can rely on Polly to cope with the pressures of dancing the lead role."

We all congratulated Polly, who was super-excited to get the part.

Leo was The Diamond Fairy. When Mum announced the cast list, she looked upset. But she didn't go off in a huff, like before. She looked worried more than anything.

Later, I knocked on Leo's bedroom door to check she was okay.

"What will my mum say?" she said, biting her lip. "I was always the star dancer at my old ballet school, and even then, I was never good enough."

"You've still got a brilliant part," I said. "And maybe

my mum can have a little chat with your mum." She seemed a bit reassured by that.

Tilda got her wish and was cast as the Lilac Fairy.

I was to be the Gold Fairy. Mum had ordered a special tutu for me, a fabulous white one with gold stitching – the nicest one of all!

The next time I was down at the flat, Mum gave me a gold box, tied with ballet-shoe ribbon.

"It's not Christmas yet," I said.

"Oh, it's just a little something special for the Gold Fairy," she said.

I untied the ribbon and opened the lid.

"Oh wow!" I gasped. It was the most beautiful tiara I had ever seen, with gold scrolls, pearls and diamantés. And under it, was a pair of gold ballet shoes.

"Mum, I love them!" I said. "Thank you."

"You've worked so well here, helping everyone to get along. You deserve them," she said.

27. Sleeping Beauty Rules!

Over the next two weeks, we worked solidly towards our performance of *The Sleeping Beauty*. Willow didn't have time to chit-chat with us any more. We were just like a professional ballet company, and we had to behave as such.

"We need to run through the finale one last time," said Willow one morning.

"This is the millionth 'last' time!" complained Tilda.

"Tilda, if you're serious about ballet, you will practise as many times as it takes," said Willow.

Now we were seeing the professional side of Willow. She didn't let us rest for a second. This was the reality of a ballet career.

"Okay, girls," said Willow. "We'll take it from the *pas de quatre*. Then onto the *mazurka* and ending with the *apotheose*!"

On the day before the Big Show, snow fell over the Cloudberry estate, making it look completely magical.

"I hope all the parents can make it through the snow," I said, looking out of the window.

"Yeah, I so want my family to see me dance the Lilac Fairy," said Tilda.

"And you don't want to be stuck here for Christmas," I said.

"I dunno, that wouldn't be *so* bad," said Tilda. "If Mrs Mathers is cooking Christmas lunch, I'd consider it!"

I laughed.

Thank goodness, the roads were clear on the day, and not only did all the parents arrive, but some of the girls who were coming to Cloudberry in the new year made it too. And there were loads of media people, who had seen the *Little Ballerina* documentary and wanted to feature us on their programmes and in their newspapers and magazines.

All Mrs McLennan could talk about was the TV show that *she* had organised and *her* little girl had starred in, which was *so* much more important than our "sweet little" school show. But underneath all the fuss she seemed very proud of Leo.

Mum told all the parents how well their daughters had done in their first term at Cloudberry and gave them all individual reports.

We were all nervous as we got ready backstage. Willow did our make-up beautifully, and Mum put up our hair in perfect buns.

As we stood in our heavenly tutus, we caught our reflections in a huge mirror. There was a collective gasp. I had to admit, we all looked beautiful.

"Beth," said Willow. "you have turned these girls out as if they're about to perform in Covent Garden. You deserve a medal. Your standards are so high, and that's why this ballet school will be such a great success."

"Thank you, Willow," said Mum. "That's very kind of you to say so. Only the best for my ballerinas."

Tilda and I couldn't wait to get on stage.

"Check out the girl in the front row," said Tilda as we waited in the wings.

"Isn't that Velvet Hughes?" I said. "Mum showed me her DVD. Makes Leo look like a little sweetheart!"

"I can just imagine," said Tilda with a smile. "But it's nothing we can't handle."

The performance was perfect. Every *glissé*, *pas de basque* and *pirouette* was of textbook standard. And as for the finale – all the effort paid off when we danced the *mazurka* scene like professionals. Polly made a wonderful Princess Aurora and the *apotheose* was really emotional. The audience seemed to love it all.

"Leo's actually dancing like a member of the team," said Tilda during one of our little breaks in the dressing room.

"Yeah, I know. Amazing, isn't it?" I said.

"I think she's much happier than when she used to hog all the glory," said Tilda.

"I agree." I smiled. It was lovely that we were all getting on so well.

During the last scene, I thought I saw Dr Campbell sitting at the back, with his blanket over his knees. I was *sure* it was him. I waved, and he waved back at me. My throat went tight, and I swallowed hard. I couldn't blub before the finale.

And then I noticed Lily standing next to him, in her ballet outfit. She waved and smiled. Her face wasn't pale and poorly now. She looked happy.

At the end of the show, we were given a standing ovation and Dad presented Mum with a huge bouquet of flowers.

"We've been a little busy this term," said Dad in his speech. "Thank heavens for Mrs Renton and Mrs

Mathers. Otherwise, we'd have been eating pickled-onion crisp sandwiches and popcorn all term!"

Madame Fussette, Willow and the wonderful Mrs Renton and Mrs Mathers were all given bouquets too. After that, I had a special presentation to make.

"Mum and Dad, we would like to present you with this picture of a little ballet dancer who used to dance through Cloudberry Castle – Lily Lamont," I said. Tilda and I had asked Mrs Renton to have the picture of Lily blown up to poster size. Between us, we told the audience the story of our discoveries about Lily Lamont.

Mum and Dad smiled proudly.

"We may not approve of all their methods of detective work," said Dad. "But we applaud their findings!"

Everyone cheered. I looked over to where Lily stood. She smiled happily, then vanished along with Dr Campbell.

Their visit to the show would have to be one of my Cloudberry secrets.

28. Old Times

Once all the girls had gone home for Christmas, and Mrs Mathers and all the other staff had gone to visit their families, Mum said we should decorate our flat and forget about the rest of the school.

"Let's make mince pies!" said Mum. "And decorate the tree. Christmas is for family. And whatever happens on the other side of the big door, family always comes first."

I smiled. "Can I dress up as Princess Aurora and dance on the stage?" I asked.

"Go on then," said Mum. "And you can show your dance to the grannies and grandpas when they arrive!"

"Cool!" I said, and dashed off to practise. I had Cloudberry all to myself once more!

On Christmas morning, my phone rang.

"Hello?" I said.

"Katie, it's Leo! I'm calling to wish you happy Christmas. I'm really missing school," said a nervous sounding voice.

"Leo, it's great to hear from you!" I said. And I meant it. I was full of Christmas feelings.

"Hey Sorcha and Hamish, come and dance with me in the studio!" I said.

"Yeah!" said Sorcha.

"Do I have to?" moaned Hamish.

"Yes, I'll make sure it's fun," I said.

When we got there, I put on a CD of *The Nutcracker*.

"Sorcha, you can be the Sugar Plum Fairy. Hamish – you're the soldier. And I'll be Clara," I said.

"Great. I love soldiers!" said Hamish. "I'll march up and down!"

We danced happily for ages.

Dad appeared at the door. "There you are," he said. "The grannies and grandpas have just arrived. Let's go and greet them!"

"Hooray!" said Sorcha. "I love Christmas. Especially because we get to see all my favourite people."

I hugged my little sister and Hamish too.

"Race you to meet the grannies!" I said.

We had a wonderful family Christmas up in the big castle. But on Boxing Day, something was on my mind.

"Mum," I said, "would you take me over to Lily's statue?"

Dad had mended the bridge, and it was much safer now, but we still weren't allowed to cross it on our own.

"Sure, I'd like to see it," she said.

We walked quietly over there, taking a bunch of white Christmas roses.

"The lake is iced over," I said.

"Yes, but it's still dangerous," said Mum.

We were very careful on the bridge.

It was easier to find the statue now that the trees were bare. Dad had agreed to tidy the island up in springtime and plant some flowers.

When we reached the statue, I placed the roses by Lily's feet.

"We'll always be ballet friends, Lily," I said.

The Wishcatchers

Carol Christie

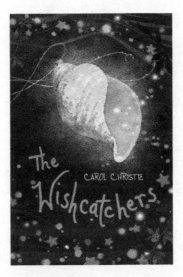

In Antonia's village, they have a special way of making wishes: they write them down, put them in a lobster creel, and row it out to Wishcatchers Point. But you need to be careful what you wish for…

This is a wonderful story of friendship and magic that will enchant its readers.

www.discoverkelpies.co.uk

Everyone loves

Janey Louise Jones

"I love your books because they are happy books and they help me understand friendship more."
Millie, aged 8

"You are my favourite author because I love reading your books. They have lots of drama and imagination. Sometimes the characters remind me of me and my friends."
Carmen, aged 7

"You are an amazing writer. I wish I was a character in one of your stories!"
Emma, aged 9